QUEENIE PEAVY

Queenie had said "I don't care" for so long and about so many things that she sometimes believed it herself.

★ "A robust portrait of a 13-year-old girl whose special talents are besting the boys at rock throwing and tobacco spitting. Queenie's everyday life in the eighth grade...takes real mettle because her father is in the federal penitentiary....When, finally, the intelligent girl who could be top of her class faces up to her father's faults...she rescues her future from reform school and starts a chain of events which reveal to her a glimpse of the warmth of family life and of rewarding work."
—Library Journal, starred review

"Queenie's emotional conflicts are well-portrayed, and the story has vitality and significance which extend beyond its immediate background of Georgia during the depression years."
—ALA Booklist

Queenie Peavy

Robert Burch

Queenie Peavy

Illustrated by Jerry Lazare

Puffin Books

PUFFIN BOOKS

A Division of Penguin Books USA Inc.
375 Hudson Street, New York, New York 10014
Penguin Books Ltd, 27 Wrights Lane, London W8 5TZ, England
Penguin Books Australia Ltd, Ringwood, Victoria, Australia
Penguin Books Canada Ltd, 10 Alcorn Avenue, Toronto, Ontario, Canada M4V 3B2
Penguin Books (N.Z.) Ltd, 182–190 Wairau Road, Auckland 10, New Zealand

Penguin Books Ltd, Registered Offices: Harmondsworth, Middlesex, England

First published by The Viking Press 1966
Published in Puffin Books 1987
25 26 27 28 29 30
Copyright © Robert Burch, 1966
All rights reserved
Printed in the United States of America
Set in Caledonia

Library of Congress Cataloging in Publication Data
Burch, Robert, 1925–   Queenie Peavy.
Summary: Tormented by taunts that her father is in prison, thirteen-year-old Queenie retaliates
by causing a lot of trouble until she discovers something important about her father and herself.
[1. Schools—Fiction. Counry life—Fiction] I. Lazare, Jerry, ill. II. Title.
PZ7.B9158 Qe 1987   [Fic]   86-30334   ISBN 0-14-032305-8

for three special friends,

Jimmie Cole
Wilda Jackson
Roxanna Austin

Queenie Peavy

Contents

Queenie Peavy

A Deadly Aim

Queenie Peavy was the only girl in Cotton Junction who could chew tobacco. She could also spit it—and with deadly aim. She could do a number of things with a considerable degree of accuracy, most of them unworthy of her attention.

"You've only been in the eighth grade a month," said Mr. Hanley, the principal of the county high school, "and already you've been sent to this office more than a dozen times. It's shocking! It's absolutely shocking!" He waited for her to reply, but she pulled at her ragged sock tops and said nothing. "And the variety of complaints about you. Why, I didn't realize girls ever did such things." Sounding as if he still couldn't quite believe the last one, he exclaimed, "Throwing rocks at the boiler-room door!"

"It made a good target," said Queenie, adding in an almost boastful tone, "and I hit the latchstring ten times out of ten."

"That's not anything to brag about."

"Why, it's a perfect score," said Queenie, surprised that he was not impressed. "And Cravey Mason only hit it twice; that's what the fight was about. He owed me a nickel that we bet on it."

"I know all that," said Mr. Hanley, "and I'm ashamed of you for throwing rocks and for gambling on it—and for fighting afterward. And I was ashamed of you on Monday when you hid in that tree and dropped a handful of chinaberries on Miss Shelby's head."

Queenie said matter-of-factly, "I didn't know it was her. I thought she was one of those prissy senior girls."

"But you don't understand," said Mr. Hanley. "You shouldn't climb trees at thirteen. Why, you're almost grown. Look at yourself, you're as tall as a woman."

"Taller than some," said Queenie.

"But you behave childishly. You know you shouldn't surprise anybody in the schoolyard by suddenly dumping chinaberries on them." He smiled and added pleasantly, "Even prissy senior girls." But his voice became sterner when he named other reasons for her being sent to his office in recent weeks. "It's a terrible list of incidents," he concluded.

Instead of appearing ashamed, Queenie looked him square in the eyes and said, "You left out one or two."

Mr. Hanley shook his head. "I don't want to expel

you. Your teachers tell me you have a keen mind and that when you take an interest in your studies it's a pleasure to have you in a class. But why do you misbehave so much?" Queenie didn't answer, and he added, "Very well, that'll be all for now."

She got up to leave and was at the door when he called out, "Oh, one more thing. Someone from the courthouse left a message that Judge Lewis wants you to come by there after school." Judge Lewis was the district judge who was in Cotton Junction for the fall term of court. He came every October for a few weeks.

"What does he want?" asked Queenie.

"I don't know. But I'd suggest you make it your business to drop by and find out."

"Yes, sir, I will," said Queenie, her voice, even her facial expression, seeming less defiant.

Mr. Hanley looked at her. "And if you think of anything that I can do to help you behave yourself, I wish you'd let me know."

Queenie scowled. "I don't care what you do about me," she said. "I don't care about anything!" And she turned and walked away. She expected him to call her back, but he didn't. And she was sorry she hadn't said something sensible. Except she had said "I don't care" for so long and about so many things that she sometimes believed it herself. So she put one hand on her hip and walked down the hall, whistling just loud enough to attract attention as she passed open classroom doors along the way.

After school she went directly to town, where she saw
Persimmon Gibbs and Floyd Speer standing in front of
the drugstore. Both boys were a year younger than
Queenie and in the seventh grade. They hung out in
town most of the time because Persimmon's mother and
father operated the café next to the post office and
Floyd's parents had a dry-goods store. "Let's go back of
the stores and shoot marbles," suggested Persimmon.

"No," said Queenie. "I've got to go up to the courtroom and see what ol' Judge Lewis wants with me."

"We'll go, too," said Floyd, telling them to wait a
minute while he told his folks where he was going. Persimmon could go anywhere without asking, but Floyd
always had to get permission. A minute later he reap-
peared, followed by his younger brother Delco, who
wanted to watch court in session also.

The four of them crossed the street, cut through the
flower beds of the courthouse square instead of keeping
to the walks, entered the rear door of the building, and
went up one flight of stairs to the big courtroom. The
back of it was crowded, and Queenie and the boys
made their way to the vacant front bench. There was no
one in the witness chair, and the judge was speaking to
twelve men sitting off to one side. "What's happening?"
whispered Delco.

"The judge is charging the jury," answered Queenie.
"Listen and find out."

Judge Lewis continued talking to the twelve men.
"And the defendant is accused then of unlawfully and,

with force and arms, feloniously breaking into the store-house and taking therefrom forty cartons of cigarettes, an unknown quantity of headache powders, and a case of castor oil." Several people laughed when the castor oil was mentioned.

Queenie looked around the room and saw that most of the people in the rows of seats were men. The majority of them were farmers in overalls, although a business suit was seen here and there. She looked toward the front again and was surprised to see that the coal stove had a fire going in it. The last few days had turned off unusually chilly for early October, but she hadn't thought of anybody needing a fire. On the other hand, she remembered that the courtroom always seemed cold and damp.

She listened again to the judge. "Now, gentlemen," he said, "this defendant has placed his character in issue, and I charge you that good character is a substantial fact and like every other fact that appears in proof should be weighed and considered by the jury. However, if it is proven beyond a reasonable doubt that . . ." He talked on, but Queenie stopped listening when Floyd nudged her.

"Look what I found on the end of the bench," he whispered, holding up half a plug of Brown Mule chewing tobacco. "Have you got your knife with you?"

Queenie reached in her pocket and drew out the rusty whittling knife she always carried. Floyd opened it and the three boys cut off a small piece of the to-

bacco. When Queenie's turn came, she closed the knife
and put it back in her pocket.

"Ain't you having any?" asked Floyd.

Instead of answering, Queenie lifted the plug of tobacco to her mouth and bit off a wad of it. "I don't need
a knife," she told him.

A few minutes later Persimmon got the hiccups. He
hiccuped loudly three or four times and then put his
hand over his mouth and went running from the courtroom. Delco whispered, "He swallowed his tobacco."
Delco himself had been smart enough not to chew his;
Queenie saw it in his hand. But she and Floyd worked
away at theirs.

When time came to spit, she waited until the judge's
attention was fixed on the jury and then took careful
aim—but not at the spittoon on the floor at the end of
the bench. Her target was the coal stove and she hit it
near the bottom, where the fire inside had burned down
to a red-hot glow. There was a crackling, spattering
noise and the judge looked across the courtroom.
Queenie sat motionless, gazing at a piece of flypaper at-
tached to a light cord. But Floyd was caught chewing.

"*Get out!*" said the judge, pointing at him. Floyd
darted from the room and the judge went back to ad-
dressing the jury.

A minute later there was another loud noise—the
same spattering on the stove—and the judge pounded
his gavel. "Who did that?" he called, looking at Delco.
"Young man, are you chewing tobacco?"

"Oh, no, sir, your Honor," said Delco. "I don't know

how." He opened his mouth wide, as if to prove there was nothing there that shouldn't have been. Some of the men in the jury box laughed.

The judge looked at Queenie. "It wouldn't be you, would it?"

Queenie touched her chest. "Me?" she said. "Oh, no, sir, your noble Honor."

The judge smiled. "I should know that a girl wouldn't do such a thing."

At that, Queenie said angrily, "There's nothing I can't do!" and she spat the rest of her tobacco onto the stove.

The judge looked at her, at first without saying a word. No one made a sound until he spoke again. "All right," he said, "you may leave now."

Queenie stood up but did not walk away. Returning the judge's stare, she said, "You sent for me."

"Come back tomorrow," said Judge Lewis, and Queenie sauntered toward the back of the room, followed by Delco trying to get her to hurry. The judge added, "And next time, come in and sit quietly if court is in session, or wait for me outside."

"I might," said Queenie, from the end of the aisle, "or I might not." She stepped quickly from the room and raced with Delco down the stairs and out onto the square. They hid in the low-growing limbs of a magnolia tree while they waited to see if Sheriff Townsend or the clerk of court or anybody would be sent to look for them.

But the only person to come along was Floyd, and they signaled to him. "Mamma's looking for you," he told Delco, and Queenie watched the two boys go across the street. Their parents' store was in the row of one- and two-story buildings that faced the south side of the courthouse square. Similar low buildings faced each of the other three sides, and that was all there was to the business part of town.

Queenie walked away from the magnolia. She thought of going over to the café to tell Persimmon what had happened after he left, but his folks didn't like anybody just sitting around without money to spend. They had told her so.

"It's time to go home, anyway," she said to herself, turning left at the end of the block. A few automobiles were parked along the side street, and horse-drawn wagons and buggies were tied to hitching rails in an empty lot behind the stores.

Big houses were next—two-story wooden ones with front porches that ran the width of them. The porch ceilings were supported by tall, white columns, a feature of these homes that were so old probably nobody could remember when they were built. In his march through Georgia during the War between the States, General Sherman had somehow missed burning Cotton Junction, sparing its houses for future generations. Unfortunately, the boll weevil had not, in later years, overlooked any part of the area. The insect had ruined the cotton-growing business that was the cause of the prosperity the region had once enjoyed.

"And now we're having a depression," thought Queenie, remembering Mr. Page's explanation in civics class about the hard times that had come upon the whole country. But the houses in the main part of town, even if some of them did need painting and had a shingle missing from a roof here and there, looked big and handsome to Queenie Peavy. She wondered what it would be like to live in one of them and was having pleasant thoughts along that line when she saw little Tilly Evans playing in the grove of oak trees in the next yard. Tilly edged nearer the front porch of her home when Queenie came in sight, then chanted: "Queenie's daddy's in the chain gang. Queenie's daddy's in the chain gang."

"He is not!" shouted Queenie. "You shut your mouth."

Tilly hopped onto the porch and hid briefly behind one of the big columns. A few seconds later she poked her head out and chanted again: "Queenie's daddy's in the chain gang. Queenie's daddy's in the chain gang."

Queenie reached down and quickly picked up two stones. Tilly dashed for the front door and barely got inside it before Queenie hit the facing with one of the stones. The noise brought Mrs. Evans, Tilly's mother, rushing from the house.

"What in salvation is going on?" she asked. "What was that blamming against this house?"

"Queenie's throwing rocks at me," whined Tilly, who had followed her mother into the yard.

Queenie said, "Well, she was saying lies about me."

Mrs. Evans asked, "And does that give you an excuse to throw stones at a seven-year-old child?"

"I wasn't throwing at her," said Queenie. "If I'd been

throwing at her, I'd have hit her. I've got better aim than 'most anybody."

Mrs. Evans turned to Tilly. "And what were you saying that made Queenie mad?"

"Nothing, Mamma," answered Tilly.

"She was saying my daddy's in the chain gang," said Queenie. "She sang it over and over."

"Well, dear," said Mrs. Evans, "she learned it from the older children. I've heard them saying it to you when you go past."

"I don't care who says it, my pa's not in the chain gang."

"Now, dear," said Mrs. Evans, "everyone knows about your father."

"Well, he's not in the chain gang," insisted Queenie. She looked straight at Mrs. Evans and continued. "He's in the pen. He's up in Atlanta in the federal penitentiary, that's where he is, and that's not the chain gang."

"It's hardly anything to brag about that his crime was a federal offense," said Mrs. Evans.

But Queenie's attention was distracted. "Hey, look a-yonder!" she said. "There's a squirrel." And in a flash she threw the other stone that she had picked up.

The squirrel, scurrying up the trunk of one of the oak trees at least sixty feet away, fell to the ground. Queenie ran to get it and a moment later returned to where Mrs. Evans and Tilly stood. She said happily, "How about that for a good shot!" and held out the dead animal.

Mrs. Evans said, "That squirrel was almost a pet. It's

been around here since last spring and would practically eat out of our hands." She added angrily, "And it was on our property."

"Well, you can have it," said Queenie. "I killed it for you, that's all." She held out the squirrel.

Mrs. Evans screamed when the fur touched her arm. "I don't want it!"

"Then I'll take it," said Queenie, calmly walking away. "Me and Mamma'll have it for our supper."

"Foolish Questions"

Half a mile beyond Hilltop Baptist Church, Queenie turned off the main road onto a wagon trail. It had originally been a sawmill road, but that was a long time ago. Now it was a rutted path. It led through the swampy low ground that Queenie called "the deep woods" and onto the open land of Elgin Corry's farm.

Elgin was one of the few Negroes in the community who owned his own land, and his family was one of the few in the county, white or Negro, to dwell in a brick home. It wasn't big, but it was brick all the same. and snug and clean and cozy-looking. Elgin had built it himself. Besides farming, he hired himself out to local builders when his crops were laid by—whenever jobs were available. A few years back, before times turned off so bad, he had bought bricks after a bumper farm crop and had encased his wooden-frame home. The house always reminded Queenie of the story of the three little pigs. It looked to her like one out of a picture book, the way it fitted onto a small rise with shade trees in front and the barnyard in back and cropland off to each side and a pasture in the distance. The whole place had a steadfast look, but most especially the brick house, and Queenie imagined that a wolf could huff and puff forever and not blow it down.

Catherine Corry, Elgin's wife, was sweeping the yard in front of the house with a brush broom, and Queenie called to her, "Howdy, Catherine!"

"Good afternoon, Queenie," came the answer, and both of them waved. Queenie continued along the trail and into a stretch of pine trees that separated the farms of the Corrys and the Peavys, the only two families that lived thereabouts.

The pine grove was on a hillside and the trail had partly washed away, becoming a shallow gully that served as a wide path. Its bright-red clay matched up pretty, thought Queenie, with the wild flowers that bloomed on each side at this time of year. There were the silvery-white rabbit tobacco blossoms and yellow goldenrod. And the purple spikes of September glory seemed to be everywhere. Queenie smiled as she thought, "It ought to be called October glory if it's gonna hang around this late in the year."

She was through the pines by then and came out onto the Peavys' land, which had grown up in weeds and

scrub bushes in the years since her father had been
gone. And the house looked neglected, too. Queenie
figured that one good huff from an angry wolf would
splinter it to pieces. But the thought had never fright-
ened her, even when she was younger. She used to
imagine herself escaping to the Corrys' brick house,
where she would get to see the wolf come flying down
their chimney and land in the boiling pot.

The front steps of the Peavy home had fallen in and
the boards on the porch had rotted away. One beam
had given way and a corner of the roof was caved in.
Queenie said to herself, "If Pa were here he'd fix that ol'
porch and we could use the front door again." She
switched to thinking of something else before it could
cross her mind that the porch had needed repair before
her father had been sent away and that a small patch-
ing job then would have held back decay.

At the kitchen door Queenie gave a gentle shove to
two hens that blocked the top step and went inside. She
laid her books on the cot in one corner of the room and
went over to the stand near the window, where she
poured a gourdful of water from a bucket into the washpan and rinsed her hands and face.

Next, she opened the cupboard and found only one
biscuit there. Punching a hole in it with her thumb, she
walked back to the table and filled the hollow with sor-
ghum syrup from a pitcher that was almost empty.
After she ate the syrup and biscuit she went out into the
yard and skinned the squirrel she had brought from

town. She rinsed the meat in several panfuls of fresh water, carried it back into the house and sprinkled it lightly with salt, and left it in a dish.

She returned to the yard then and drew another bucket of water. She was pouring part of it into a can that served as a chicken watering trough when she heard someone coming through the pines. It was eight-year-old Dover Corry, singing "Foolish Questions." She recognized his voice. He was coming along the path from his home and was most likely being followed by Avis, his five-year-old sister, and their dog Matilda. That was the way they usually traveled.

Queenie quickly hid on the opposite side of the well. When Dover came to the end of one of the verses, Avis joined in on the chorus:

> "Foolish questions.
> What is there to say?
> Foolish questions.
> You hear them every day."

Dover sang another verse as they walked into the Peavys' back yard, and Avis was joining in on the chorus again when Queenie jumped out screaming from behind the well, waving her gangly arms over her head. She ran after Dover first, and when he darted behind the henhouse she turned and chased Avis. Avis ran squealing into the pines, then back to the well. Only Matilda, the hound, remained unexcited. She stood where she had been when the commotion started, probably seeing no sense in falling for the same trick over

and over. But Dover and Avis ran back and forth across
the yard and in and out of the edge of the woods, always just a step or two ahead of Queenie, who pretended to be trying awfully hard to catch them. She
chased first one and then the other until Dover, who
had dodged behind one of the biggest pines, called,
"We give up!"

Avis echoed him, "We give up!" and both of them
came strolling into the yard, out of breath and giggling.

"How come you to scare us like that?" asked Dover,
and Avis, echoing him as always, repeated it. "How
come you to scare us like that?"

"Just like to hear you whoop and holler," said Queenie,
sitting down on the steps. Avis sat down beside her, and
Matilda ambled over and put her head in Queenie's
lap. "Hello, Matilda, you ol' pot-liquor hound!" said
Queenie. "Have you been climbing any trees lately?"

Matilda gazed up as if she understood the question
but chose not to answer it. Dover said, "I saw her clear
up in the top of a poplar this morning about day-
break."

Avis said, "Why didn't you call me? You promised
that next time you'd call me."

"You weren't awake," said Dover.

Avis turned to Queenie. "Dogs can't climb trees, can
they? Dover's making all that up, ain't he?"

Queenie said, "Most dogs are not climbers, but Matilda's not like most dogs." She winked at Dover.

"That's right," said Dover. "Matilda can do all sorts
of things because she's part fox."

Avis said, "Last time you said she was part bobcat."

"But I meant fox."

"Foxes can't climb trees," said Avis proudly, as if she had finally disproved their stories.

"The kind of foxes Matilda comes from can do 'most anything," said Dover.

Queenie asked, "Do you know that big sweet-gum tree down by the spring?"

The children nodded that they did.

"Well, I saw Matilda sitting up in the tiptop of it the other day, alongside three foxes. But I didn't know they were kin to her."

"Probably her first cousins," said Dover, and he and Queenie grinned at each other while Avis whined that they were all the time seeing things she didn't get to see and that they kept promising over and over to call her next time. They were assuring her that they would certainly do better about it in the future when a voice from across the pines called, *"Dover! Avis!"*

They answered together, "Coming, Mamma," and Dover turned back to Queenie. "I forgot to tell you what we came for. Mamma says can she borrow two eggs. She's making us a chess pie."

"I'll get 'em," said Queenie, going into the kitchen. But the shoe box that served as an egg container was empty. "We'll have to look for some," she said when she got back to the yard.

The nest boxes along the wall of the henhouse were checked first. "Here's one," she said, handing the egg to Dover. They went next to the apple crate that was nailed onto a wall of the Peavys' home. Standing on a big rock in order to look into the crate, Queenie said, "Nothing here but the nest egg." She held up the chipped porcelain doorknob that was supposed to lure the hens into laying their eggs in the nest instead of in hidden locations. Turning it over in her hands, she asked, "Reckon your ma could use it in a pie?"

Dover and Avis laughed, but Queenie's voice became serious. "There ought to be more eggs somewhere. I wonder what's wrong with the chickens."

"Maybe they're molting," suggested Dover.

"Our hens got more sense than that," said Queenie. "They molted in late summer when they were supposed to."

While she led the way to other nests, Dover explained that his mother's hens were molting but that it was not because they lacked intelligence. He insisted that it was because they had been hatched in the wrong season and had been off schedule ever since. He was still defending them when Queenie came across the one more egg that was needed. It was in the small keg that rested between the forked branches of a peach tree.

By then Dover and Avis had been called four times from across the woods. Each time they had joined voices to reply, "We're coming, Mamma," and when the two eggs had finally been located they started home. Avis said, "We mustn't dilly-dilly on the way."

"Dilly-dally," corrected Dover as he hurried along the path, followed by Avis, followed by Matilda.

The yard was quiet again and the chickens gathered

in close to Queenie, reminding her that it was time for them to be fed. "Only two eggs today!" she scolded. "I'm a-good mind not to shell you a grain of corn." She looked over the flock—two dark red hens, three white ones, five with black-and-white-barred plumage, and a buff-colored one. In addition, there was Ol' Dominick, the rooster, who came by his name because he appeared to belong to the barred breed called Dominique. "None of you look sick," said Queenie, walking to the edge of the house. She pulled a burlap bag of corn from under the corner of it and took out two ears, which she began to shell by turning one crosswise of the other and rubbing down on it. She scattered the corn across the yard and when there was nothing left but the cob of the first ear, she pressed it against the other one until it, too, was shelled. The chickens scurried about the yard in search of each kernel that hit the ground.

Queenie shelled four ears in all and then sat down on the steps to watch the chickens finish their meal. Afterward, the hens stood about for a few minutes, the way chickens do when they're hoping for more of a handout, then gave up and wandered off into the weeds in search of seeds and insects to supplement the slim ration they'd been given. But Ol' Dominick came and hopped onto the steps beside her.

She stroked his neck and back and he made a pleasant sort of gurgling noise and pecked at her hands.

"I'm not gonna give you any more corn," said Queenie. "What makes you think you deserve anything

extra?" He repeated the throaty sound and she added,
"You know I'm just teasing. I always save you a few
extra grains, don't I?" She opened her hands and he began to eat the corn she had held back for him. When it
was gone he made a clucking sound.

"Why, thank you for asking me," said Queenie. "I'd
be pleased to sing you a song."

Ol' Dominick clucked contentedly, as if that's what
he was hoping she would do. Because the tune of "Foolish Questions" was still in her mind, she sang it in a clear
contralto voice. Queenie could sing well, but few people
had ever heard her. In school she was always too busy
showing off, pretending she didn't care about anything
or anybody, to join in on song sessions. And when a
teacher asked her every now and then to do a solo on a
program, she would choose not to cooperate. But in her
own back yard, sometimes with Dover and Avis and
sometimes right by herself with no one but the chickens
listening, she felt comfortable singing out.

"There's only one more verse of it," she said to Ol'
Dominick, and he cocked his head to one side and listened to the words:

"There's a busybody woman who will meet you on your
        way,
    She'll ask you where you're going and she'll listen while
        you say,
You're going to the funeral of your poor old Uncle Ned.
    And sure as life she'll ask you if your Uncle Ned is dead.
Foolish questions,

You might as well reply:
'No, he thought he'd have the funeral first—
    then later on he'll die!' "

At the end of it, Ol' Dominick cackled loudly, then
flapped his wings and crowed.

"Well, thanks," said Queenie. "I'm glad you enjoyed
it."

Ol' Dominick hopped from the step onto the hard-
packed ground of the yard as if he knew the show was
over. But instead of walking away, he turned and flew
back onto the step beside her and pecked at her hands
again. She opened them wide for him to see that supper
was over, too. "Haven't you heard?" she said. "Nobody
around here gets enough to eat."

The Sweet Potato

Town students went home for lunch every day. Bus riders from out in the county and those who walked a goodly distance, such as Queenie, brought their lunches with them. At the twelve o'clock bell they unwrapped sandwiches, or whatever they had packed, and ate in their homerooms. When they were finished, the teacher on hall duty would let them go outside to play or walk around the schoolyard until time for classes to begin again.

Queenie told the eighth graders—the ones who were at their desks having lunch—about being caught chewing tobacco the day before. They all laughed, especially at the part about Persimmon getting the hiccups and swallowing his wad.

Melvin McWhorter confessed, "I don't expect I could

have done much better. One time my brother Grady and I bought us a plug and we both got sick from it. I don't see how anybody chews the stuff."

"There's nothing to it," said Queenie, not saying that she had made up her mind never to try it again, even to show off. The taste it left in her mouth was awful and it made her stomach hurt, besides. She would just think of other ways to prove how tough she was.

The girls in the room said they didn't envy Queenie *all* her talents, but they wished they could catch on to algebra the way she did. "Civics, too," added Kate Coogler. "I never can keep it straight about who does what in all those capitols and things in Washington, D.C., that it takes just to run a country." That led into a discussion of the debating topics Mr. Page had assigned during the morning and what grade each one had made on the surprise test of the day before.

Cravey Mason, whose grades were never a matter he cared to talk about, said, "I've got a good baked sweet potato that I'll trade off."

Nobody ever had much more in their lunches than they needed, but every now and then they swapped around whatever they did have. "You can have this for it," said Cressie Whitfield, holding up an apple.

Cravey took it and examined it. "Nope," he said, handing the apple back to her. "It's afflicted."

"It's got a wormhole," said Cressie, "if that's what you mean. But when did you get so finicky?"

Cravey asked, "Anybody else have anything to offer?"

"I'll give you the bread part of this pig-in-a-blanket," said Leroy Wheeler.

"No, but I'll swap for the sausage," answered Cravey. Leroy's views on that proposal were made clear when he began eating the roll and link sausage.

Other students suggested what they would swap for the potato, not sounding as if they were really interested in it. But Queenie hadn't had any sweet potatoes so far this season and the baked one looked good to her. She said, "Cravey, I'll swap you a sandwich for it."

"Are you crazy?" he said. "You don't have any sandwich. All you've got is a biscuit and sowbelly."

Little Mother, whose real name was Martha Mullins, spoke up. "That's a sandwich; of course it is. What else could it be?" She was always trying to keep things running smoothly among her friends. That's why they called her Little Mother.

Queenie said, "And besides, I didn't say that's what I had."

"You didn't have to say it," answered Cravey. "It's all you ever have." He turned up his nose. "Biscuit and sowbelly!"

Little Mother said, "You should say 'home-grown bacon.'"

"Call it anything you please," said Cravey "—side-meat, fatback, city chicken, streak-o'-lean-streak-o'-fat, or whatever. But I ain't trading my potato for any of the lousy stuff."

Queenie said angrily, "Who asked you to?"

"*You* did."

"I said a sandwich. You don't know what's in it. And anyway, I've changed my mind." She lifted the biscuit, and a rind of the fatback stuck out from between the two halves of it.

"I knew it," said Cravey, laughing loudly.

"I happen to like *home-grown bacon*," snapped Queenie. She bit into the biscuit and began chewing noisily, smacking her lips.

Little Mother started telling about how some folks considered fatback a delicious treat. She said, "My father's cousin knew somebody who moved up north to New York City and couldn't find any of it to suit her. She kept asking for fatback in the stores and at first they didn't know what she was talking about."

"How come?" asked Cressie.

"Well," said Little Mother, "it turned out that they called it salt pork, but even then it wasn't as good to her as the kind that we cure. So her family took a side of meat out of their own smokehouse and wrapped it up and mailed it to her." Kate Coogler giggled as Little Mother continued. "And besides that, they sent her a box of grits every now and then, too, because she couldn't find them any place up there either."

"Those folks must not know what's good," said Hank Franklin. "It's pretty poor doings not to have grits."

Grace Rogers shrugged her shoulders. "Oh, they're crazy up there, anyway."

"Why, no," said Little Mother, "we shouldn't feel that

way just because they happen not to enjoy everything
we like. And I feel sure they have some things that we
don't know about."

"Probably nothing good," said Grace, and Little
Mother said, yes, they probably had things that were
very good that might just be real interesting to discover,
and that she hoped they, in turn, kept an open mind
about whatever anyone else had. Queenie decided that
Little Mother not only wanted her friends to get along
with each other but was now promoting good will and
understanding for the whole world.

Just then Mrs. Thaxton, the teacher on hall duty for
the week, looked into the room. "If you've finished eating," she said, "you may go outside."

The students got up from their desks and began filing
past the trash basket to throw away their lunch wrap-
pings—all except Queenie, who remained in her seat.
She wadded up the sheet of newspaper that had contained her lunch and threw it over everybody else's
head. It landed in the basket.

She complimented herself heartily. "Good shot,
Queenie-girl!" she said. "It's a pleasure to know somebody with good aim!"

Mrs. Thaxton called out from the doorway, "Now,
Queenie, you know better than to do such a thing. Just
for that, I want you to stay right in this room while the
others go outdoors."

"How come?" asked Queenie.

"I've just told you why," said Mrs. Thaxton.

"If I'd missed the basket," said Queenie, "all you'd have done would have been to say: 'You march yourself up to the front of this room and put that paper in the trash can where it belongs!'" She tried to imitate the way Mrs. Thaxton would have said it, and her classmates snickered. "You're punishing me for being a good shot," she continued, "and it's not fair." She put one hand over her heart and waved the other one in the air and said loudly, "And much it grieves my heart to see what man has done to man." She was slightly misquoting from a poem, "Lines Written in Early Spring," that had been read at the assembly program the afternoon before.

"Now don't get sassy," said Mrs. Thaxton, "or I'll report you to the principal."

Queenie started to say something else but changed her mind. She sulked while the rest of the students hurried outside. Cravey Mason called from the corner of the room, "I threw my potato in the trash, Queenie. If you want it bad enough you can fish it out."

"I don't want a thing you've got," said Queenie.

When everyone had left, Queenie went to the trash can and dug out the sweet potato. She took it and walked over and stood by the window. "I'll show Cravey Mason a thing or two," she said to herself.

Every day after lunch the boys kicked a football back and forth on the schoolyard, and Queenie knew that frequently bad aim landed it on the walk beside the building. She was certain that sooner or later Cravey

would come near the window to retrieve the ball. When
he got in range, she planned to give a shrill whistle to
get him to look in her direction, and then she would
hurl the potato at him with such speed that he wouldn't
have time to dodge it. And with her aim, she knew she
could hit any target dead center. She was smiling at the
thought of it when she heard someone walk into the
room. Before she could look to see who was there, the
football hit the walk and she watched to see who would
get it. When Joe Moore ran after the ball, Queenie
turned back toward the room.

Little Mother was walking toward the front desk. "I
came back," she said, stopping at the trash can. She
reached inside it and began to shuffle the papers about.
"I thought that if you meant what you said about not
eating the potato that . . . well . . . that I'd just have it
myself. I'm still sort of hungry."

Queenie held up the potato. "I've got it," she said. "I
beat you to it."

"Oh, that's quite all right," said Little Mother, apolo-
getically. "I just didn't see any need of it going to waste,
but it's quite all right if you've decided to eat it."

"I have *not* decided to eat it," said Queenie flatly.
"And I'm surprised that you would consider having it
yourself. Don't you claim any pride?"

"Why, of course I have pride," said Little Mother,
sounding a bit dumfounded. Her voice became high-
pitched as she continued. "But I don't have foolish
pride. Why, the potato hasn't even been peeled. It's

perfectly clean and good, and as I said, I happened not to be too full from what I had for lunch and I just thought that——"

Queenie interrupted her. "I'm going to hit Cravey Mason square in the middle of his stupid face with it."

"Why, that would be awful!"

"It'll serve him right," said Queenie, "for saying what he did about my lunches." She looked straight at Little Mother. "And another thing, you didn't need to come to my rescue with a lot of silly talk about home-grown bacon. I can look after myself."

Little Mother laughed nervously. "Why, I wasn't coming to your rescue any more than my own." She blew at a strand of hair that had fallen in front of her eyes. "I have the same lunch you do 'most every day, only some days I don't get but one biscuit in mine. I have six brothers and sisters who have to have lunches to bring, too, and all of them are littler than I am—except Dave." She paused to ask, "You know Dave, don't you? He's in the ninth grade."

"I know him," said Queenie, not letting on that she especially liked him and wished she knew him better.

"But the rest of the children in the family are younger than I am," continued Little Mother, "and if there happens not to be two biscuits around when I'm fixing the lunches, I usually let them have a bit more than I take." Her voice became more motherly than ever and she sounded for all the world like a grownup talking. "I figure they're little and need to grow—and me being

thirteen and all, well, I don't require too much." She
looked at the potato. "But I do think it's sinful to waste
food."

"Oh, all right," said Queenie. "Here, eat it. Maybe
you'll choke to death."

"Why, thank you," said Little Mother, quickly peel-
ing the potato. "My, it's baked just exactly right."
Breaking off part of it, she said, "You must have half;
it'll make you feel better."

Queenie accepted it, scowling; she had never realized
that Little Mother helped at home with a house full of
children. Maybe that's how she came to act so growny.
They were each taking a bite of potato at the moment
the football landed on the walkway again. Cravey Mason ran to get it, and after he picked it up he peeked in
at the window.

"Well, well!" he said, grinning broadly and looking at
what the girls were eating. "Having a picnic?"

Little Mother said pleasantly, "It's awfully good. Are
you sure you wouldn't care for part of it?"

Cravey's grin disappeared. It seemed to make him
mad that he had been greeted with an invitation instead
of an angry response. He started away, then turned back
to them. "Scavengers!" he said in a low tone. "That's
what you are. Two scavengers—a possum and a turkey
buzzard!"

Night Work

The kitchen of the Peavys' house was as big as the other room. A wood-burning cookstove occupied one corner of it. Next to the stove was the woodbox and then the cupboard and then a plank bracketed to the wall to serve as a shelf. The shelf held pots and pans and milking utensils. Queenie's bed, a cot that also served as a seat, was pushed against the opposite wall. At one end of the room there was a small stand that held the kerosene lamp. At the other end, a low bench holding a washpan and water bucket occupied the space near the back door. A nail in the wall held the gourd dipper, and a second nail served as a towel rack. In the middle of the floor were a pine table and two straight-backed chairs.

The other room of the house was where Mrs. Peavy

slept. In addition to an iron bed it contained a rocking chair and a dresser with a high mirror cracked from one side clear across to the other. Whenever Queenie looked at herself, which was not often, she either stooped down or stood on her toes in order that the crack would not split her face in two. Also in Mrs. Peavy's room was the wardrobe, a large piece of furniture with drawers on one side and a place to hang clothes on the other.

And those were the only two rooms of the house. A galvanized laundry tub in the yard near the washpots was brought indoors for bathing, and the rest of the bathroom facilities, other than the washpan, consisted of an outdoor wooden toilet.

Queenie stayed in the yard most of the time, even in October. In the afternoons after she got home from school she would find the sunniest spot, usually near the chimney on the west side of the house, and get on with her studying. The day the debating topics had been assigned in civics, she became so absorbed in what she was reading that she was sorry when she had to quit. But the long shadows of the walnut tree nearby warned her that the time had come to do the night work.

"I wonder why it's called night work," she asked herself as she went inside to put away her books. "The chores are late-afternoon ones and yet everybody around here calls them night work."

She thought more about it while she gathered the eggs. "Maybe it has to do with getting the work done before night catches you," she concluded, and began to sing, "Work, for the Night Is Coming," although she realized it had nothing to do with afternoon chores. Or maybe it did, in a way, she thought. "In the song, you're supposed to be working and accomplishing what you can while you're alive because someday you're gonna die." She sang over a few lines that bore out the moral:

> "Give every flying minute
> Something to keep in store;
> Work, for the night is coming,
> When man works no more."

"At the same time," she said, "some of the words sure do seem to fit these short days we have in the fall and the chores I have to get done before the sun goes down." She sang the last verse while she chopped kindling at the woodpile:

> "Work, for the night is coming,
> Under the sunset skies;
> While their bright tints are glowing,
> Work, for daylight flies.
> Work till the last beam fadeth,
> Fadeth to shine no more;
> Work while the night is dark'ning
> When man's work is o'er."

Ol' Dominick, who had kept a safe distance from the chopping block, crowed approvingly at the end of the song. "Well, thank you," said Queenie, "I'm happy to know that you like a hymn now and then." She stopped and fed the chickens their ration of corn, then took the kindling and the eggs into the house, where she got down a milking pan and bucket from the shelf.

As she walked along the path through the pines she hummed "Ring, Ring the Banjo" until she came out at the pasture gate. The cow was not there and she walked on to the Corrys' barn. Elgin Corry had let the Peavys shelter their cow in his barn since their own shed had fallen over. They, in turn, let Elgin's cow and his two mules graze in their pasture, which had more grassland than his.

At the barn, Queenie called, "Elgin, are you in there?"

"I'm here," came the answer from inside. "So is Sweetheart." Sweetheart was the Peavys' cow. "She was at the gate and I drove her up when I brought in Amaryllis."

"Well, I'm going on to your house and draw some water," said Queenie. "I forgot to bring any." Water was always used to rinse dirt from the cow's udder before the milking began.

"There may be a little left here," answered Elgin, and Queenie went inside. Elgin, on a milking stool at the side of Amaryllis, reached out to a bucket on the doorsill of the next stall. "No," he said, "I must have poured it out."

Queenie walked across the barn lot and into the Corrys' back yard. A half-filled bucket of water was on the well and she poured a small amount of it into her pan.

Catherine greeted her from the kitchen doorway and

asked, "If you see anything of Dover out around the barn, would you send him to bring in a load of stove-wood, please?"

"I'll see him and Avis both. They supervise me while I milk. Want me to tell him he won't get any supper if he doesn't come help you?"

Catherine laughed. "It might be a good idea. And if that doesn't work, try telling him we're having smothered chicken."

Queenie asked, "Are you, sure enough, or is that just a joke?"

"We are, sure enough," said Catherine, pressing out her apron with her hands. "That late drove of biddies I raised has come in mighty handy."

"I'll round up Dover for you," said Queenie, heading toward the barn calling at the top of her voice, "Dover! Dover Corry! Dover-Dover-Dover-Dover-Corry! Where are you?"

"*Boo!*" shouted Dover and Avis, hopping out at Queenie from each side of the barnyard gate.

"I knew you were there all the time," said Queenie, not missing a step on her way toward the barn. "Your ma wants you, Dover."

"What for?"

"To give you a whipping!"

"What for?" This time it was Avis who asked.

"For scaring me," said Queenie, "while I was walking along, minding my own business, and not doing a blessed thing to you."

The children giggled. It was evident from Queenie's

tone that she was teasing about the whipping part. "But your ma does want you. She needs a load of wood right away."

"Don't tell her you saw me," said Dover, starting off in a different direction.

"She's cooking a chicken," said Queenie.

"Then maybe I'd better go haul in the wood. But I'll be right back." He called over his shoulder, "Milk slow!" as Avis and Queenie entered the barn, where Avis hurried to climb onto a partition wall overlooking the cows.

Elgin had finished his milking and was untying fodder from the feed room to give to the mules. "I think the cows have been eating wild onions again," he said. "The milk tonight smells like they have."

"Maybe it won't show up in the taste," said Queenie, knowing from experience that when cows grazed on such things as wild onion or bitterweed the milk was sure to contain a trace of the flavor. "If it's not one thing, it's something else," she concluded.

Elgin smiled. "That's the way of it. But we wouldn't know how to act if it wasn't."

Queenie slapped Sweetheart on the flank to get her to move her right leg back far enough to begin the milking. She told Elgin, "Cold weather ought to kill the onions."

He shivered. "That's an awful price to have to pay for better-tasting milk. Cold weather—brr-rr! I think I'd rather have wild onions, wouldn't you, Avis?" He swung one arm around his daughter and swept her off her perch. "Come on," he said. "It's time for you and me to go eat supper."

Queenie wished it were time for her to eat supper, too, but she knew it would be a long time yet. Her mother did the cooking at their house and she hadn't gotten home from work.

When Queenie got back to the kitchen with the milk she strained it, using a clean cloth over a wire strainer that doubled as the flour sifter. Then she set about making a fire in the stove. She put wadded-up paper on the grate, covered it with pieces of pitchy pine kindling, and laid stovewood on top. She struck a match and held it to the paper, which blazed up quickly. The kindling, rich in resin, caught fire from the paper and crackled as it burned, giving off an agreeable smell. "I'm a good fire-builder," said Queenie, "if I do say so myself." She turned the damper on the stovepipe at an angle to cause more air to be pulled through. The increased draft made the fire burn even brighter and the chunks of stovewood were soon ablaze. Queenie then closed the damper partially, not wanting the wood to burn away too fast.

She pulled out one of the chairs from the table and started to sit down but remembered suddenly that the stovewood she had used had been the last the box near the window contained. "Work, for the night is coming!" she told herself, walking out into the dusk to bring in an armload of wood from the pile near the chopping block.

Inside the house again, she took the kerosene lamp from the stand at the end of the room, lit it, and put it in the center of the table. Then she got out her English book and began to read, but she had difficulty concentrating on the rules of diagraming when the events of the day kept crossing her mind. That Cravey Mason! She would get even with him yet! The way he had treated her and Little Mother at lunch time was bad enough, but his insult during algebra in the afternoon had been even worse. It came when Mary Nolan had knocked on the door and Mr. Waldron had asked from across the classroom what was wanted.

Mary, a tenth-grade girl who worked in the office during sixth period, replied, "Mr. Hanley said to tell Queenie Peavy that Judge Lewis will not be at the courthouse any more this week and he left word for her to come see him next Tuesday."

"Thank you," said Mr. Waldron, and Mary left, but there was a stirring among the students. "You heard, didn't you, Queenie?" asked Mr. Waldron.

"I heard," answered Queenie.

Cravey Mason said in a voice low enough so that perhaps Mr. Waldron could not understand him from the front of the room, "Maybe the judge is gonna send Queenie to jail, too." The other students had heard and laughed, which had been the part that hurt most.

"*Make Cravey shut up!*" yelled Queenie.

"Now, Queenie," said Mr. Waldron, "calm yourself and tell me what he said."

Queenie hung her head. "I couldn't hear it," she mumbled.

"Then don't get angry about something you didn't hear, but I do want everybody, including you, Cravey Mason, to be quiet and listen to what I have to say." At that he returned to the lesson—multiplication in solving equations—and Queenie began thinking of what she would say to Cravey when the class was over. But when the bell rang Mr. Waldron asked Cravey to stay behind.

Queenie thought about it while she sat at the table, waiting for her mother to come home. Maybe Mr. Waldron had heard Cravey's remark after all and had kept him behind for a good scolding. She hoped so. Or maybe she didn't hope so. Maybe Mr. Waldron didn't know about her father being in prison. Maybe there was somebody somewhere who didn't know. Mr. Waldron was new in the school this year; maybe he didn't know all about her the way everybody else seemed to. She hoped he hadn't heard what Cravey said and that he hadn't known why some of the students laughed. Then he wouldn't be nice to her because he felt sorry for her. She knew that at times she was pitied, and that made her almost as mad as anyone saying mean things about where her father was.

But there were some people who didn't pick on her and who seemed not to pity her, either. They were the ones she genuinely liked. Kate Coogler was such a person, and so were Floyd Speer and Little Mother and Little Mother's ninth-grade brother Dave—most especially, Dave. He always seemed natural and friendly.

She liked him, and she cared for other people, too. But Cravey Mason was no good, and she hated him and all the other girls and boys who teased her. Besides hating them for what they said, she hated them for what they made her say and do. And if she only wouldn't make matters worse by trying to cover hurt feelings by pretending nothing mattered. She was still brooding over it when she heard the rustle of dry leaves in the yard, and knew her mother was coming. She began hoping her mother would be in a cheerful humor. Maybe something funny had happened at the cannery today. It would be nice to hear something funny.

The back door opened and Mrs. Peavy came into the kitchen. "Well, howdy-do," she said pleasantly.

"Howdy," said Queenie, looking down at the open English book as if she had been studying it. "Did anything jolly happen at the canning plant?"

"Not a thing," said her mother, taking the gourd dipper and filling it with water. "It was an awful day. We were busy every minute and we had to work late besides." She drank a sip of the water, then said, "I hope you've seen to things."

"I've milked," said Queenie.

"And gathered the eggs?" asked Mrs. Peavy.

"Wasn't but three. I don't know what's got into those chickens."

"Probably the cold snap," said Mrs. Peavy. "They ought to do better in a day or two." She walked over to the churn that sat on the floor in the corner and began untying the cloth that covered it. "I suppose you've done the churning already," she said, looking inside the big earthenware vessel. "What's this? The milk hasn't been churned yet and I'm sure it must have been clabbered hours ago."

"I forgot to look," said Queenie, getting gawkily to her feet. "I'll do it now." She took down the dasher from the plank shelf.

"I don't know what's gotten into *you*," said her mother. "You used to be so smart around the house." She lifted the breadboard and tray from the bottom of the cupboard and set them on the table.

"I'm still smart *around* the house," said Queenie. "It's inside it that's where I fail!"

Mrs. Peavy smiled but continued her lecture. "I know you're growing up and all that, but we still have to eat. And I work my fingers to the bone at the canning plant, and on the days I have to work extra hours it does seem that you'd do a little more than is absolutely necessary. It wouldn't even hurt you to make the biscuits and have them rolled out before I get home."

"Me make biscuits!" said Queenie, as if it were the most preposterous suggestion anyone had ever offered. "Say, Mamma," she added, "I've got a good idea for us! Let's start eating store-bought bread."

Mrs. Peavy looked at her. "I do believe the recent cold snap addled your brain," she said, already pouring milk into the flour tray to start the dough. "Just what do you think we'd use to pay for it?"

"Money," said Queenie, with a harsh laugh, and Mrs.
Peavy smiled. "I know," continued Queenie, trying to
sound like her mother, "where'd we get the money for
anything that's different from what we always have?"

"We're lucky to have flour to make our own bread,"
said Mrs. Peavy, while Queenie dragged the churn
across the floor to a spot nearer the lamp. "And besides,
those boughten loaves are not much good. They've got
no more body to them than a wad of cotton—and not
much more taste."

"I don't recollect ever tasting cotton," said Queenie,
laughing as if she had made the best joke in the world.
Mrs. Peavy laughed, too, and began humming "What
Can You Do with a Sawed-off Shovel?" a lively square-
dance tune.

Queenie churned in time with the song; and the fire,
poked up now to get the stove hot enough to bake biscuits and fry fatback, crackled away. The room seemed
pleasant and cozy. Queenie thought how much nicer it
was with two people in it—and that it would be even
nicer if there were three. She could picture it clearly in
her mind because she had done it often. It was her favorite thought: the dream of her father being home
again.

The Trick on Cravey Mason

"This would be a good day for our field trip," Mr. Hatfield announced at the beginning of the science lesson the next afternoon. Outside the window the sun was shining and the few clouds that were in the sky were a long way off.

"Yes, sir," said Melvin McWhorter enthusiastically, "it sure would!" And Joe Moore agreed, "It's a *fine* day for a field trip."

"But I thought we were going to the woods next time," said Kate Coogler.

"We are," said Mr. Hatfield. "That's our field trip this time."

"Oh," said Kate, "I thought field trips were just when you went to fields and meadows." Everyone laughed, and Kate laughed with them.

"We went to fields and meadows last time," explained
Mr. Hatfield, "because we were studying plants that
grow there. But now that we're studying mosses and
ferns we'll dip into the woods." He motioned toward
the wooded area across the road from the school building. Smiling, he added, "But if it's confusing to you,
Kate, we can call today's trip a woodland escapade.
Come along, let's be going before I change my mind."

Everybody hopped to their feet and followed Mr.
Hatfield from the room. Little Mother, walking beside
Queenie as they crossed the school grounds, chattered
all the way. "I just love field trips, don't you? At home
we're so busy all the time that I never seem to have a
chance just to stroll around."

"I play in the woods all the time," said Queenie.

Little Mother continued, "I do love trees and wild
flowers and birds and everything so much that it would
seem I'd spend more time among them. After all, I live
in a remote rural area."

Cravey Mason, a few steps ahead, overheard the conversation. "Remote rural area!" he said. "Is that a new
term for 'the sticks'? You know that you live so far out
in the country it ain't nothing but the sticks. How come
you to put on airs?"

Queenie said angrily, "Mind your own business, Cravey Mason!"

But Little Mother answered him pleasantly. A nerv-
ous giggle was the only indication that she might be
upset. "Why, Cravey, I didn't mean to sound affected.
It's just that it seems almost disrespectful of nature not

to use a dignified term for countryside that's so beautiful."

Instead of answering her directly, Cravey yelled out: "Hey, everybody! Guess where Little Mother Martha Mullins lives. She lives in a *remote rural area.*"

"All right," called Mr. Hatfield. "Simmer down back there."

Queenie whispered to Little Mother that she would get even with Cravey and for her not to worry about it, but Little Mother insisted she had not been offended. She babbled on about how boys will be boys, as if she were an old woman.

The class stayed close together when they first got into the woods. Some of the students, instead of trying to help Mr. Hatfield locate plants of special interest, threw pine cones and berries at the ones who were ahead of them. Little Mother tried to coax everybody into behaving. "Maybe we'll get to come more often," she said, "if we conduct ourselves properly."

As usual, the troublemakers paid no attention to anyone advocating good behavior, but they did listen when Mr. Hatfield told them to stop lagging behind. A few minutes later he had everyone gather around him to examine an example of a bracken fern.

While they stood there, a bird lit in the top of a buckeye tree across a small clearing. Mr. Hatfield asked, "Does anybody know what kind of bird that is?"

Hank Franklin said, "It's a jailbird," and everybody laughed—all except Queenie. Whether jokes were aimed at her or not, any mention of jail was automatically taken as a personal offense.

She said angrily, "It's a brown thrasher, and Hank Franklin knows good and well that's what it is."

Little Mother raised her hand and Mr. Hatfield asked, "Yes, Martha?"

Little Mother said, "The brown thrasher is my favorite bird."

"Mine, too," said Mr. Hatfield. "Have any of you ever heard its song?"

Queenie said, "I bet I can hit it with a rock from right here." She jumped onto a tree stump and drew back her arm to throw a stone.

"*Stop that!*" said Mr. Hatfield. "Don't you ever kill a brown thrasher!" He lectured briefly about birds that should never, under any circumstances, be killed. "But let's get back to ferns and mosses," he told them. "I want everybody to look for an example of each." Pointing toward a stream that was to be the boundary line, he added, "And don't anybody cross the creek. I'll blow the whistle in five minutes and I expect all of you to come running."

The students started off in various directions. Cravey walked close to Queenie and whispered, "Just can't do anything right, can you?" He tried to imitate her voice: "*I bet I can hit it with a rock from right here.*"

Queenie whirled around, and Cravey jumped behind a sweet-gum tree. He poked his head out on the other side and chanted, "Queenie Peavy, Puddin' and Pie!"

Cressie Whitfield, a few yards away, finished it: "Kissed the boys and made them cry."

"No," said Cravey, "but how about, 'Throws rocks at birdies in the sky?'"

"It rhymes," said Cressie. "Queenie Peavy, Puddin' and Pie, Throws rocks at birdies in the sky."

"Jailbirdies!" said Cravey, laughing hysterically. And the madder Queenie got the funnier it was to him and to some of their classmates.

Mr. Hatfield called, "All right, over there, break it up! Scatter out and find those examples."

Queenie walked away and Little Mother followed her, saying, "Don't let them upset you. Boys—and girls, too, lots of times—don't mean nearly all they say."

"They didn't upset me one bit," declared Queenie defiantly.

"Good," said Little Mother. "And just look at this little tree somebody chopped down but forgot to haul away." The end of the tree was resting on its own stump.

Queenie was out near the other end, where the branches had been cut away. "It's just a sapling," she said. "The sawmill crowd probably couldn't use it." At that, she started up the thin log, saying she always had liked walking on rails. She had taken no more than four or five steps when the larger end of the log slipped from the stump and crashed to the ground. Queenie fell to one side.

"Are you hurt?" asked Little Mother.

"Just lost my balance," said Queenie, getting up.

"Lucky it wasn't nearer this bank," said Little Mother, looking down the steep drop to the stream.

"Say," said Queenie, "that gives me an idea." She lifted the smaller end of the rail-like log and pushed it over until it was parallel to the bank. "Here, quick, help me lift the big end," she said, and Little Mother obeyed her. They propped the base of the log back onto the stump, with only a slight overlap to hold it.

"Why, that's dangerous," said Little Mother, standing back to look at what they had done. "What if someone should try to walk up it the way you did, not realizing that it was barely balanced on the stump?"

Queenie laughed. "They'd be more careful next time."

"But they'd fall down the same as you, and if they toppled the wrong direction they'd go into the creek."

"Aw, it wouldn't hurt 'em," said Queenie, "the water's shallow." And she began calling loudly, "Cravey! Cravey Mason! Come over here and see what we've found!"

In a very few seconds Cravey, followed by Hank and Melvin, were at the creek bank. Queenie said, "I'll bet you can't walk up this rail."

"Nothing to it," said Cravey, starting up the log.

"I don't think you should try it," said Little Mother. "It could be dangerous."

"You think everything's dangerous, Little Mother, except fishing sweet potatoes out of trash cans," said Cravey, taking careful steps up the log like a tightrope walker. And at that moment Queenie reached out one foot and gave the base of the log a kick.

Cravey swayed to the left toward the ground, then

swerved back to the right and fell over the bank, landing in the stream. His knees buckled and he sat down in the water.

Everyone on the bank laughed and Queenie taunted, "What are you doing splashing around in the creek? This isn't the time of year to go swimming," and everybody laughed again.

The small end of the log had landed in the water near Cravey, but the heavier end of it was hanging on a mass of roots and vines near the top of the bank.

Cravey got to his feet and waded out of the stream. He grabbed hold of the vines and started to pull himself up the steep incline. But in tugging at the vines he pulled them loose from the entangled roots, and the heavy end of the log fell into the creek bed. The end of it struck his left leg near the ankle and he fell backwards into the water, yelling loudly.

The rest of the class gathered around, and Mr. Hatfield hurried over. "Cravey Mason!" he said. "What are you doing down there?"

Queenie said, "He's taking his Saturday-night bath on Friday afternoon. That's how crazy he is."

Cravey tried to stand up, but his left leg gave way. "My foot's hurt," he said.

"Then don't try to use it," said Mr. Hatfield, sliding down the bank. He waded into the stream and helped Cravey to the edge of it, where they both examined the injured foot.

"Maybe you'd better not try to walk," said Mr. Hatfield. "If somebody will help me, we'll lift you back to the schoolhouse."

"Let me!" said Leroy Wheeler, who was the biggest boy in the class. He jumped into the shallow water before anyone else could volunteer, and he and Mr. Hatfield, by clasping each other's wrists, formed what they called a "side saddle." It served as a seat for Cravey, and slowly they made their way downstream to a spot where the bank was not steep. There they were able to get back onto higher ground.

On the way out of the woods, nobody laughed and talked the way they had earlier. Almost nothing was said until they got to the edge of the road and heard the school bell ringing. "Time for last period," said Mr. Hatfield. "Leroy and Cravey and I can't move fast, but the rest of you must hurry. Don't be late to your next class or we'll all be in trouble."

Queenie and Little Mother entered the building through a side door, and by the time the second bell sounded were seated in algebra class. It was not easy for Queenie to concentrate on the lesson, even though she especially liked math. She kept thinking about what had happened and hoping that Cravey wasn't really hurt.

When school was out, Mary Nolan called to her from the office door, "Mr. Hanley wants to see you first thing Monday morning."

Several eighth graders crowded around and Queenie asked, "Why doesn't he want to see me now? If he's got a sermon to preach, he's not one for putting it off."

Mary said, " 'Cause he's gone to take Cravey Mason to the doctor."

A student who had not been on the science field trip asked, "What's ailing Cravey?"

"Mr. Hanley thinks it's a sprained ankle, but he wants the doctor to check."

Mary and the other eighth graders went on their way —except for Little Mother. She said, "Don't brood over it too much, Queenie. You were just playing a trick on Cravey, you didn't mean to cause him any harm."

Instead of admitting that Little Mother was right, Queenie said, "Of course I meant him harm. I hope he broke his leg."

"*Them Promises I Never Ever Kept*"

Mr. Hanley was in his office when Queenie knocked at the door. "Come in," he called.

She stepped inside. "Mary Nolan told me Friday that I was supposed to see you this morning."

"Yes, I was expecting you. I'll be with you in a minute." He continued to examine typewritten pages that were spread out in front of him. "I don't know," he said at last, "I just don't know! Maybe you can tell me what it will take to get you to behave yourself." He took a paperweight from a drawer and placed it on top of the papers, then turned to her again. "Have you any ideas?"

"About what?"

"About getting you to behave. Sit down and think about it while I go ahead with my work." He opened a letter, read it, and put it under the paperweight. He unfolded a circular next and threw it in the wastebasket. Then he asked, "Have you thought of anything yet?"

"What time is it?" asked Queenie.

"Now what has that got to do with——"

Queenie interrupted him. "I didn't want to cause you to miss ringing the first bell."

"That's my department," he said, "and I'll do my best to manage it." He looked at his watch. "But it is time for the bell. Would you mind ringing it for me? It's there behind you." Queenie pressed down firmly on the button that was fastened to the wall. She let it ring for a long time. "Whoa!" called Mr. Hanley, smiling at her. "It's a school bell, not a fire alarm."

She released the button and asked, "Can I go?"

"Keep your seat," he said. "I want to hear your version of Friday's accident. I've already had Martha Mullins in here and interrogated her." He went over the details Little Mother had told him about the injury to Cravey's leg. "Now is that the way it happened?"

"Even if it weren't," said Queenie, "I don't imagine you'd believe my side of it. Can I go now?" She got up and Mr. Hanley's face turned red. He looked at her sternly and she sat back down. "Now, Queenie, of course I'll believe you if you tell the truth."

"How can you tell whether I tell the truth or not?"

"I'll investigate until I've got all the evidence that it's possible to obtain."

Queenie said flatly, "Little Mother told the truth."

"What?"

"Martha Mullins. She got it straight. You can believe her."

"Then you deliberately laid the trap that caused the accident," he said. "You're a problem and you've left me no alternative but to bear down on you." He shook his head slowly. "One more of your misdeeds and I'll have to expel you. Is that clear? Just one more thing. You've left me no choice."

"Yes, sir," said Queenie.

"There's something else I want to say," said Mr. Hanley, "and it doesn't have to do specifically with Friday." His voice became softer. "I understand that some of your classmates aggravate you at times with references to your father's status."

Queenie said angrily, "My father's status is none of their business!"

"That's what I want to get across to you," said Mr. Hanley, "it's none of their business. And, also, it's not of their own doing that they themselves have been more fortunate than you. As for the ones who are so unconcerned about your feelings that they make jokes, well, you must learn to consider it their own sadness instead of yours." He looked at Queenie, but she was fidgeting with the corner of her notebook and did not lift her head. "I know it's hard to take at times and I'll do my best to curb it—and don't think for a minute that teachers and principals don't always know more about what goes on around a school than you realize. But you can make my job easier. In fact, you could make things easier for you and me: Why not ignore unkind comments and pokes? Students who annoy you would get tired of it if you gave no response to their provocations. Will you do as I suggest?"

Queenie did not look up, but he waited for an answer. At last she said, "I'll try. I'll pretend it's their sadness instead of mine."

"No," he said, "you misunderstand. You don't have to pretend. It *is* their own sadness if they are crude enough to tease you, and sooner or later they'll realize it. None of us ever knows when we'll be caught up in situations we'd rather have avoided, but one thing's certain: when we are we don't want anybody to laugh at us. It's then that we'll wish we'd been more understanding of others. Do you see my point?"

"Yes, sir, I guess I do."

He continued, "I'm firmly convinced that people who are inconsiderate hurt themselves in the long run more than they hurt anyone else." He looked at his watch. "You may go now, but think about what I've said. Also, I want you to promise to apologize to Cravey when he gets back to school. All right?"

"Yes, sir, I promise."

"And when I've decided on appropriate punishment for Friday, I'll send for you and Martha."

"Me and Martha!" said Queenie. "What's she got to do with it?"

"She aided you. She told me she helped you prop the log back on the stump in its precarious position."

"She lent a hand, but she didn't know what I was up to. Then when she did, she tried to talk me out of it. You can't punish her."

Mr. Hanley said, "That's not for you to decide. But I'm glad to hear that Martha hadn't known what you were planning. I didn't think it was in her nature to ever want to hurt anyone."

Instead of getting to her feet, Queenie leaned back in her chair and asked, "What's so terrible about a sprung ankle, anyway? Plenty of folks have 'em."

Mr. Hanley put down a letter he had started to open. "*Sprained* ankle, not *sprung*," he said. "And Cravey does not have a sprung, or rather, sprained ankle."

Queenie laughed at his near misuse of the word himself, but her smile disappeared when he added, "I thought you knew—Cravey's leg is broken."

That was the first she had heard about it. She had gone directly to the office when she arrived at school and had not talked with anyone beforehand. But when she got to English class she learned that Cravey's leg was the subject of everybody's concern. Little Mother said, "Isn't it just too unfortunate the way things turned out?"

"Yes," said Queenie flatly, "it's too bad."

Little Mother whispered, "But I know you didn't really mean to hurt him. I know you didn't mean what you said and I promise I've forgotten it already and you needn't worry about me repeating it to another living soul. I know you didn't really wish he broke his leg."

Queenie looked over at her friend. "Maybe he'll die," she said. "Wouldn't that be a good joke on me and you?"

Little Mother looked horrified. "Queenie! You know you don't mean that!" Before Queenie could answer, Mrs. Thaxton came into the room and the lesson got under way.

Cravey returned to school the middle of the next morning. Queenie saw him when she went into the auditorium for study hall, but she did not stop to talk. Other students had gathered around him and were looking at his cast.

"How much did it cost?" asked Joe Moore.

"I don't know," said Cravey. "The doctor's gonna send the bill to Queenie."

"You're crazy," said Queenie, who had taken her usual seat three rows away. "It's not my leg."

"Daddy said he was gonna see that you and your mother pay the bill."

"No need to come bothering Ma," said Queenie, not looking up. "She doesn't have any money."

Cravey threatened, "She better get up some or Pa'll send Sheriff Townsend out there to see about it."

Queenie turned toward him and forced a laugh. "That'd be just like your pa to do that!" Cravey's father had the reputation of being extremely tightfisted with money and uncooperative in many ways. Queenie started to add a few more insults but it came to her that she was doing the very thing she hated in others: ridiculing a member of someone's family.

Cravey said, "Daddy's already told Dr. Palmer to send the bill to your house."

Mr. Waldron came into the auditorium and stood at the end of the aisle. He did not have to say a word; the students knew what was expected of them and they went to their seats and sat down. Nobody talked or cut up during one of Mr. Waldron's study halls.

Queenie tried to work on her English assignment, but her thoughts kept going back to the doctor's bill that Cravey had mentioned. "Why did they have to bring Ma into it?" she asked herself. She brooded about it for the rest of the morning.

At lunch time she did not join her classmates in their conversation—most of which had to do with a detailed report by Cravey of how the doctor had set his broken bone and how the cast had been applied. When it was almost time to go outside, Queenie remembered her promise to apologize to Cravey. She got up from her desk, tossed the newspaper wrapping from her lunch into the trash can, and walked across the room. She stood near Cravey's desk and began, "I want to say something."

"Sure," he said, "you want to say you'll write all of us a letter from jail." Grace Rogers and Hank Franklin laughed, and Cravey continued. "Maybe they'll put you and your mother in the same cell with your pa. Is that what you want to say?"

Queenie looked at him coldly. She was about to go ahead and apologize until Grace and Hank laughed again. Cressie Whitfield joined them, and Queenie looked at all three, a hurt expression on her face. Then she turned back to Cravey and told him, "All I've got to say is that if you don't leave me alone I may decide to break your other leg, too!" At that she marched toward the door, only to meet Mrs. Thaxton head-on. "May I go outside?" asked Queenie, a trace of anger still in her voice.

"Certainly," answered Mrs. Thaxton pleasantly. "Everyone who has finished eating may go outside."

After school Queenie passed Mr. Hanley's door and saw him moving chairs into his office for the regular Tuesday faculty meeting. She wondered if he knew she hadn't kept her promise to apologize to Cravey. She wondered if it would be the *one more thing* to cause him to expel her. In a way she hoped it would. She hated school. Not really, not the lessons. Just the people, and she admitted it was only certain ones of them she didn't like.

She met Dave Mullins running to catch his bus. Even in a hurry, he waited to let her walk in front of him instead of causing her to have to jump out of his way. She did not dislike him. But all those others, or to be more honest, only some of those others, were no good. She hated them, and she hated herself for always making matters worse. She asked herself as she walked along why she couldn't learn to take everything in stride.

She answered silently, "Because Pa's in the penitentiary and I get mad when anybody touches on the subject." Something seemed to add, "Yes, and you're too hotheaded and stubborn to think before you act. You do make matters worse on yourself."

"So what?" she asked whatever corner of her mind had produced such reasoning. "You don't really think that when anybody insults me I'll stop and consider that silly idea about it being their own sadness. No siree, I'll slap 'em in the face if I have the chance." She was angry when questions kept arising in her own mind to try to persuade her that Mr. Hanley had been right. One minute she would resolve to do better; the next, she would think back about something spiteful someone had said and get mad all over again.

She couldn't convince herself that she had always been in the right whenever she got into scraps. It made her mad to admit it and she picked up a handful of stones along the roadside and began throwing them at whatever caught her eye. She knocked a cone from a loblolly pine tree, topped a stalk of goldenrod in a meadow as neatly as if it had been cut by a bullet, and sank a stone into a knothole on the highest branch of a hackberry tree. She hit everything she tried to hit.

On the outskirts of town a redbird flew across the road in front of her. It lit in the side yard of the parsonage of the Hilltop Baptist Church. Queenie drew back her arm to throw a stone at it, but the bird flew over to an althea bush. Queenie took aim again. "Cardinal," she said, "I'll just spare you on account of Mr. Hatfield calls you 'a fine feathered gentleman.' But you ought not to present yourself as such a good target!" At that, she threw the stone at the base of the branch and the redbird flew away, no doubt wondering what had come over the althea bush.

Beyond the parsonage, almost directly in front of the church, there was a high bank with a cavelike hollow inside it. Queenie threw a stone at a gnarled root near the top of it and was surprised when the stone was thrown back onto the road. "Hey, who's there?" she called, not advancing farther until Persimmon Gibbs stepped out from the hollow. "What are you doing out here?" asked Queenie. "You live on the other side of town."

"Just hanging around," said Persimmon. "I've got tobacco. Care for some?"

Queenie answered, "I've quit chewing. I don't like the taste of it."

"This is smoking tobacco," said Persimmon, holding out a nickel bag of Bull Durham.

"I'll try it," said Queenie, and she walked on up and crawled into the hollow of the bank with Persimmon, where they sat and clumsily rolled a cigarette each. After striking seven matches to get them lit, they heard a door slam and looked out to see Mrs. Morganson, the minister's wife, leaving the parsonage and walking down the hill. "Wouldn't she be surprised," said

Queenie, "if she knew two children were sitting in this bank smoking cigarettes?" Persimmon laughed appreciatively and they puffed away until the hollow was so smoky that they each gasped for breath. Coughing loudly, they stumbled onto the road.

Waving smoke away, they were relieved to see that Mrs. Morganson had not turned back. Persimmon looked at the tobacco. "Smoking it is about as bad as chewing it," he said.

"Worse," said Queenie. "But thank you just the same." And she left him and went ahead home.

In the back yard Ol' Dominick was courting a hen near the well, spreading his wings in front of her and hopping about stiff-legged. It was not clear whether he was trying to entertain the hen with a dance step or merely seeing that she did not walk away. He lost interest altogether when he spied Queenie, and ran to meet her. "Go back to your girl friend," she told him. "I'm not going to feed you till later."

But he followed her inside the house and jumped onto the table. He was pecking at the broken handle of the sugar dish by the time Queenie settled her books onto the window ledge. She walked over and put one arm around him and lifted him from the table. He made his pleasant gurgling sound and she said, "All right, we'll get the song book down this time," and with her free hand she took down the book from on top of the cupboard, slapped it against her side to remove flecks of flour, and went out to the back steps.

She set Ol' Dominick down beside her, but while she

turned the pages he hurried back into the house and
hopped onto the table again. Queenie retrieved him
once more, this time closing the door when she came
out.

"Now let's see," she said, having a seat on the bottom
step. "How would you like to hear 'Chilly Water'?" Ol'
Dominick's reply was a short cackle, and Queenie said,
"All right, if you're not in the mood for that one, I'll
try 'Whoopee, Whoopee, Here Comes Flo.' It's nice
and lively." She began then to sing, and when she came
to the end of the first verse, a voice nearby chimed in
on the chorus. Avis peeked out from around the corner
of the house. Queenie stopped singing and asked, "How
did you get over there without me seeing you?"

"We came the front trail so we could slip up on you,"
explained Avis. "Dover's hiding on the other side."

Dover came out from behind the big rock that supported the opposite corner of the house. He looked
disgusted. "Aw, Avis," he said, "how come you to tell? I
was gonna jump out screaming in another minute."

Queenie flipped through the book. "You wouldn't
have surprised me the least bit," she said. "I knew all
the time you were there." Then she added, "Here's
'Them Promises I Never Ever Kept.' Let's you and me
sing the verses, Dover, and Avis, you come in on the
crying part."

They began then to sing the mournful song of a man
who had lived to regret having lied to his mother
when he was a boy, to his sweetheart when he was a

young man, and to a number of other people as well.
When they came to the chorus Avis joined in with a
shrill "Boo-hoo-hoo, oh, boo-hoo-hoo" at just the right
place, pretending at the same time to be brushing tears
from her cheeks. She became so enthusiastic about her
contribution that she carried it into the second verse,
becoming so loud and shrill that Dover and Queenie
sang at the top of their voices to try to drown out her
"Boo-hoo-hoo, oh, boo-hoo-hoo." Ol' Dominick quietly
hopped from the step onto the yard and strode off into
the weeds.

Halfway through the third verse, which had to do
with the man's lying to a judge and a jury and a courtroom full of spectators all at the same time, Queenie
slammed the book shut and jumped to her feet.

Dover wanted to know what was the matter, and
Avis asked, "Did a bee bite you?"

"I suddenly remembered," answered Queenie, "I forgot to go see the judge." Handing them the book, she
said, "Sing on if you want to, but I've got to hurry back
to town or I'll be in hot water sure enough—if I'm not
already."

The Accusation

Queenie ran into the courthouse and up the stairs to the courtroom—but the entrance doors were locked. She hurried back to the first floor and knocked at the ordinary's office. Perhaps the judge was there.

"Come in," came an answer from inside, and she pushed the door open.

"Is Judge Lewis here?" she asked.

The ordinary looked up from a big register. "I haven't seen him since lunch," he said. "You might try the clerk of court. He's at the end of the hall."

Queenie went to the last office. The door to it was open and a man was locking the big vault at one end of the room. "Judge Lewis waited for you till quarter of an hour ago," he told Queenie. "You might find him over at the jail talking to the sheriff or he may have left town. Court's adjourned for the rest of the week."

At the jail, Queenie saw Sheriff Townsend in the side yard, talking to Roy Ellins, his deputy. She walked out to where they stood and asked, "Have you seen Judge Lewis?"

"He's gone," said Sheriff Townsend. "What did you want with him?"

"He wanted to see me," answered Queenie, starting to walk away.

"Wait a minute!" said the sheriff. "I don't know what he wanted with you, but I know what I do."

Queenie turned and glared at him. "Pa's not in your jail," she said angrily.

"This is not about your pa, Miss Spitfire," said the sheriff. "It's about you. You've got some explaining to do."

Queenie was silent for a few seconds, then she said softly, "I didn't mean to break Cravey Mason's leg. It was an accident."

"This is not about Cravey Mason's leg either," said the sheriff, "although that's been reported to me, too. This is about the Hilltop Baptist Church."

The scowl left Queenie's face and she appeared more relaxed. "I pass the church every time I come to town and every time I go home. Ask me anything you want to know."

"I intend to," said Sheriff Townsend. "Why did you break out the windows in the bell tower?"

"You mean somebody broke out those windows?" said Queenie. "Well, how about that?"

"Not *somebody*," said the sheriff. "*You!*"

"Wasn't me," said Queenie, "but I wonder who it could have been." She turned to Deputy Ellins and explained, "Those windows are little bitty ones and way up high, too. Whoever hit them was a good shot."

He said, "You're noted for having good aim. We hear you're the best rock-thrower around here."

"Well, thank you," said Queenie. "I didn't know everybody realized it." She smiled proudly. "But I have to admit it's pretty much the truth."

"That you knocked out the windows?" said Sheriff Townsend.

"No, that I'm the best rock-thrower in these parts. I wish I could tell you who knocked out those windows, but I don't know a thing about it."

"You don't seem to realize one important point. You've been accused of doing it, and we've got evidence."

"You don't have evidence that I did it," said Queenie assuredly. "Because it wasn't me."

Deputy Ellins told her, "Persimmon Gibbs said it was."

Queenie's mouth dropped open. "He what?"

Sheriff Townsend nodded his head, a satisfied smile on his face.

When Queenie spoke again, she said, "Persimmon's lying."

"You did see him this afternoon, didn't you?" asked the sheriff.

"Yes, I ran into him along about the church."

"That ties in with what he told us. And you didn't know he saw you knock out those window panes, but he hadn't gone off the way you *thought* he had."

"I left ahead of him," said Queenie.

Deputy Ellins said, "Even before that, several folks saw you picking up rocks and throwing them at everything you came across."

"I always throw rocks."

"Mrs. Morganson, the preacher's wife out there, said she saw you throwing at a cardinal at the edge of her yard. She said she'd watched you from the window of the parsonage and had been relieved that you missed the redbird."

Queenie looked indignant. "I wasn't aiming at it," she said firmly. "If I'd been aiming at it, I'd have hit it."

Deputy Ellins frowned. "Most folks believe that if a redbird lights in front of you it's a sign of good luck. Anyway, you ought never try to kill one."

"Well, it's no crime to scare 'em," said Queenie, "and that's all I did. Can I go now, or are you gonna put me in jail?"

Sheriff Townsend spoke again. "We don't want you in jail," he said. "You'd be just another mouth to feed. Go on home; we'll let you know when we've decided what to do with you."

In the school office the next morning during second period, Mr. Hanley said, "Now tell me first why you didn't apologize to Cravey. You promised me you would."

"I started to tell him I was sorry," answered Queenie, "but I never did."

"Doesn't your word mean anything to you?"

"I meant to apologize," said Queenie. "I was going to tell him that I was genuinely sorry."

"I regret that you didn't," said Mr. Hanley, "but most of all I'm sorry about the extra trouble you've gotten yourself into."

"What extra trouble?"

"Breaking those windows in the church tower."

"I didn't do it," said Queenie.

Mr. Hanley continued, "And even though that's not a school problem, I'm sorry to hear you've got into more trouble."

"How'd you hear about it?" asked Queenie.

"Mrs. Johnson called from the sheriff's office a few minutes ago. It seems that Cravey's father has reported the accident that took place on the field trip the other day. In fact, he's threatening to carry the matter into court if you and your mother refuse to pay the doctor's bill. But the concern about the church windows, and the possibility of a vandalism charge against you, have brought on the immediate action. I don't know what's on Sheriff Townsend's mind, but he had Mrs. Johnson checking on your conduct record here at school."

"What'd you tell her?"

"You're intelligent, Queenie," said Mr. Hanley, looking her straight in the eyes. "What do you suppose I told her?"

"I suppose you told her that I'm intelligent!" said Queenie. She knew the answer disappointed him and added slowly, "No, I suppose you told the truth. I reckon you said I caused you a lot of trouble and that the sheriff ought to lock me up or something."

Mr. Hanley smiled. "I told the truth, but I certainly didn't recommend that you be put behind bars. I haven't given up on persuading you to behave yourself. I have a feeling that underneath your rough surface you're all right."

Queenie cocked her head to one side and asked, "What rough surface?" At the same time she brushed back her hair, remembering that she hadn't bothered to comb it since the day before. Then she picked at a torn place in her jumper that she had been planning to mend.

Mr. Hanley said gently, "No, it's not your physical appearance that worries me. If you primped the way the other girls do you'd outshine them all, but the rough surface I spoke of is the impression you try to give of not caring what happens to you. I can't bring myself to believe that you're as unconcerned as you seem to want everyone to think you are."

"I didn't break those windows," insisted Queenie. "Not that I couldn't have knocked them out. Why, I could hit a mosquito on the very top of that bell tower if I wanted to."

Mr. Hanley smiled. "That's better than Annie Oakley could have done—and she had a rifle!"

"I ought to get me a rifle," said Queenie, "or a shotgun. Then maybe folks would leave me alone and not be all the time accusing me of something." She said once again, "I didn't break those windows!"

"Didn't you?"

"I never have lied to you, Mr. Hanley. I mean, not outright. I admit I've gone back on promises to behave and I didn't apologize to Cravey the way I said I would, but I never have tried to lie out of anything once I was caught. Even about the accident that broke Cravey's leg, I——"

Mr. Hanley interrupted her. "I have a feeling you're telling me the truth. I usually can sense it. Now calm down and tell me why the sheriff thinks you were the vandal."

Queenie told the whole story of the afternoon before: the trip home, meeting Persimmon on the way, and later, her return to town and the visit with Sheriff Townsend and Deputy Ellins. Mr. Hanley listened to all of it and at the end said, "You better go; it's almost time for the bell."

Queenie, starting down the hall, rounded a corner and saw Cravey talking to someone near a side entrance to the building. The other person stepped outside the door before Queenie got there, and she figured it had been the janitor. "What are you doing at this end of the building?" she asked Cravey.

"Slipped out of study hall," he answered. "Told Mr.
Waldron I had an overdue book to take back to the
library." He laughed at the joke.

Queenie didn't think it was funny and reminded him,
"The library's at the other end of the hall."

"That ain't my fault," said Cravey. "And besides,
what business is it of yours what I do?"

Instead of getting mad, Queenie said, "I've been
wanting a chance to tell you that I'm genuinely sorry
about your leg. I apologize for causing the accident."

"You'll do more than that," said Cravey. "I told you
I'd get even with you. You're pretty certain to be sent
off to a reformatory, did you know that?"

"Who said so?"

"My daddy. He says you'll be *put away* when the
sheriff gets through investigating you. There'll be evidence a-plenty to bring you to trial. Besides breaking
my leg, now you've gone and busted out those church
windows." He laughed heartily. "Too bad about all that!
I hope I'm on hand to see you get arrested."

Just then Queenie noticed the janitor of the school
at the opposite end of the hall. Then who had been
talking to Cravey? She looked down at the partially
opened door and saw the heels of someone's shoes. She
pushed the door open and went outside.

Persimmon Gibbs stood there. "Persimmon!" she said.
"Why are you hanging around? This isn't your building." Persimmon was in the seventh grade in the grammar school next door.

"I came over at recess to meet Cravey."

Cravey stood in the doorway, then hobbled into the yard. Leaning on his crutches, he advised Persimmon, "Don't tell her anything! She's not your boss and you don't have to do any explaining to her."

That seemed to bolster Persimmon's courage and he told Queenie, "It's none of your business what I'm doing."

"I may make it my business," she said, starting away. "I think I'll go tell Mr. Hanley that you're out here."

"Aw, don't do that," said Persimmon. "Don't get me in trouble."

Queenie turned back to him. "I won't if you'll tell me why you lied to the sheriff."

Cravey said, "You don't have to tell her a thing." The bell rang at that moment and he continued, "Quick, get back to your room. The halls over here will be full of everybody changing classes and you can make it before Queenie gets through to Mr. Hanley's office." At that, Persimmon ran off in the direction of the grammar school.

Queenie did not rush back inside; she held the door open for Cravey to get through on his crutches. "Not that Mr. Hanley will believe you," he said, "but I guess you'll run tell on Persimmon for being off limits."

"I ought to," said Queenie. "But I'm not a rat."

She hurried to her locker, took out the book she needed, and went on to civics class. And even though she was late getting to it, everyone in the room was

milling around as if the second bell hadn't rung. She
thought perhaps Mr. Page wasn't there. Then she saw
him standing over one of the desks near the window.
"What's happened?" she asked.

Sue Meade said, "It's Little Mother."

"What did she do?"

"She passed out cold," answered Sue. At the same
time Hank Franklin said, "She fainted dead away."

A Helping Hand

Queenie helped Mr. Page get Little Mother to the dressing room of the stage, which doubled as a first-aid room. Miss Shelby, who was holding study hall in the auditorium, came along, too, and gave advice. "Stretch her out flat," she directed. "And Queenie, prop her feet up on the pillow."

Mr. Page disappeared and was back in a moment with a glass of water. "I sent word to the office for someone to call a doctor," he said as he dampened a cloth and sponged off Little Mother's face.

"She's all clammy," said Miss Shelby, "and so pale. Do you think we——?"

Before she finished the question, Little Mother opened her eyes. After blinking several times, she asked weakly, "What happened?"

"You fainted," answered Queenie. "Would you like a drink of water?"

"No, thank you," said Little Mother, "I'm fine now," but she closed her eyes again.

When the doctor arrived, he got her to whiff ammonia and she sat up on the edge of the cot. "I'm able to go back to class now," she said.

"*I'm* the doctor," said Dr. Palmer, smiling. "Maybe you'd better let me decide what you're able to do." Then he told Miss Shelby and Mr. Page, "I want to take her to my office for a more thorough examination." Turning to Queenie, he asked, "Could you go along to help get her there?"

"If Mr. Page says I can," answered Queenie.

"Certainly," said Mr. Page. "I'll report to Mr. Hanley where you and Martha have gone."

At the doctor's office, Queenie sat in the reception room and waited. She hoped everything was going to be all right. Various other patients had arrived while she had been sitting there—and some of them had already been treated and were gone—but Little Mother was still inside. Queenie put down the *Woman's Home Companion* she had been reading and reached for a copy of *Country Gentleman*. But a man reached for it at the same time and she pretended to have been more interested in a ladies' magazine that was beside it. She took it up and flipped through the pages, glancing up whenever anyone new entered the room, until she came to a story called "The Barriers to Moonlight," with a caption that proclaimed it an unforgettable love story. She didn't recall that she had ever read a love story and decided to see how this one started off. She knew she wouldn't like it. But after two paragraphs she was so interested in what would happen next that she hurried to read more. It was all about a rich girl who lived in a big city and her boy friend, who lived in the big city, too. Only he wasn't rich and that was the trouble. Even though he was hard-working and intelligent and ambitious, along with being handsome and pleasant-natured, the girl's father wouldn't consent to their getting married. He said he would cut his daughter off without a penny of his vast wealth if she continued even to associate with the young man. Besides not being rich, the boy did not have any socially prominent ancestors, and that didn't please the girl's family either. Queenie was relieved that in the end everything worked out exactly right: the boy received a nice promotion at his job, the girl announced that she would marry him, and her family stopped objecting to the match and planned the wedding. Her father even said he hoped his new son-in-law would come help manage the family fortune after the honeymoon, which was to be a three-month trip to Europe.

Queenie sat and thought about it. While reading, she had sort of visualized herself as the girl, thinking from the start that she certainly would have put more faith in the young man than in money and background. She

would have married him without giving the matter a
second thought, she decided, but that might have been
because she pictured Little Mother's brother Dave as
the young man. She imagined him and her boarding a
big ship, just like the one in the magazine, and waving
to that multitude of friends who had gathered on the
dock to watch them sail away. She could just see Kate
Coogler and Cressie Whitfield and Leroy Wheeler, and
all the eighth graders from out in the county, after
they'd grown up and gone to the city, turning up to
see her and Dave off. And everyone would envy her.
Even though they'd be prosperous by then, too, they
probably wouldn't have been to Europe the way she
was about to go—on account of her father having his
vast fortune and all. She was thinking about it when
someone said, "Isn't that a good story?"

Queenie looked up. She had not seen the thin, little
elderly woman come in and sit down in the chair next
to hers. They both glanced at the magazine, which
Queenie had opened to the page where the story began
in order to see the picture again. The woman said, "I
read it last week when I was in here. I just *love* love
stories, don't you?"

"Yes, ma'am," answered Queenie. "I like 'em a lot."

The woman whispered, "I always imagine myself
trading places with one of the main characters. Have
you ever done that?"

"No, ma'am," answered Queenie, "I don't believe I
ever have."

"I've never read but one story I didn't like," said the woman. "It had a sad ending and I thought it was perfectly terrible. Wouldn't you have thought so, too?"

"Yes, ma'am," answered Queenie. "Stories ought to end happy." The woman was smiling in agreement when Dr. Palmer motioned to Queenie from down the hall.

"I've given your friend a liver shot," he told her, "but she's still shaky and I want her to lie down a while longer. Why don't you go in and cheer her up?" He pointed toward a door along the corridor.

Inside the small room, Little Mother was resting on a couch. She said, "I don't know what got into me that I fainted the way I did."

"You couldn't help it," said Queenie. "What did the doctor say was the matter?"

"Oh," said Little Mother, "he thinks I'm anemic because of malnutrition."

Queenie was startled. "Malnutrition! Why, that's the same as starvation!"

"Oh, no, not at all," said Little Mother. "Dr. Palmer said it meant I wasn't getting everything I need in the way of nourishment, but I'm certainly not starved. Why, goodness gracious, we've had just plenty of things to eat. Well, actually, we've had almost enough of . . . well, several things . . . field peas and, why, I can't think of what else right now. But we haven't gone hungry—at least, not really."

"Maybe you ought not to use your strength talking," said Queenie.

But Little Mother chattered on: "Of course it's true
that we had bad luck with hog-killing. Pa knew at the
time that it wasn't too wise to slaughter one of the hogs
on the very first cold snap, but we did sort of need it.
And he had no way of knowing it would turn off warm
again so soon and the meat would spoil. And it's unfortunate that our cow picked this very time to go dry."
She chuckled, as if she were trying to give the impression that she had thought of something really amusing.
"Isn't it funny the way cows have of going dry at the
most inconvenient times? But she'll freshen any day
now, and pecans will begin to fall soon, and we'll kill
another hog when it turns off cold again, and then it'll
be time to make hominy, and my goodness, we'll be
having more to eat than we know what to do with."

The doctor said, "But that hasn't helped you in recent
weeks!" Neither girl had realized he had come back
into the room and that he had heard any part of Little
Mother's conversation. He said, "I wish you'd tell your
father about the welfare surplus food program. They
have various kinds of food, including beef and raisins,
that contain the iron you need, that they give to people
whose luck isn't running well."

"It's been discussed at home," said Little Mother,
"but Pa and Ma are against accepting aid if we can
possibly get along without it."

"Why?" asked Dr. Palmer.

"They look on it as a handout and say that folks
ought to get along on their own."

The doctor shook his head. "With the poor crops

made around here this year, and the hard times, it's not shameful in the least to accept help."

"Pa's heard about a new outfit that lends money to farmers," said Little Mother, "and he's already applied for a loan. They help farm folks such as us and will maybe provide money to feed us through the winter and stake us to seed and fertilizer next spring. That's the kind of helping hand Pa would accept, since it couldn't be confused with charity."

"All the same," said Dr. Palmer, "welfare has the extra food now, and I want you to tell your father about it." Before he could say more, the nurse rushed into the room. "Come quickly," she said. "There's an emergency!"

Queenie hopped up and ran with them. A two-year-old child had cut his hand on a jagged tin can and blood was pouring forth. The young mother, having gotten the little boy that far, suddenly was overtaken with a spell of hysteria. The doctor told the nurse to stay with her and asked Queenie to come hold the child while he doctored the hand.

The boy screamed while the wound was being cleaned and bandaged, and he yelled even louder when he was put onto a table for a tetanus shot. Queenie held him firmly while the shot was given, then lifted him onto her lap. "Don't be scared," she said soothingly, and the baby slowed down on his crying until the doctor picked up the hypodermic needle once more. At that, the boy screamed again. "It's all right," said Dr. Palmer,

"I'm putting it away." He dropped the needle into a pan to be cleaned and resterilized for future use. "Maybe you can calm him," he told Queenie, "while I see if his mother has gotten over her shock."

With the doctor out of the room, the baby whimpered for a few minutes and then stopped. Queenie patted him gently all the while. He squirmed in her lap at first, then snuggled close and was asleep when his mother came to get him.

Queenie returned to the room where Little Mother was resting, and in a few minutes the nurse brought in a tray of food. "The doctor had lunch sent over for both of you," she said. She pulled a table to the center of the floor and set the tray on it. "The patient needs a nice meal for strength," she said pleasantly. Turning to Queenie, she added, "And you deserve a treat for lending us a helping hand."

Later in the afternoon the doctor drove the girls back to school in time for Little Mother to catch the bus home. He instructed her about special foods to eat and when to take the pills he had given her, and he thanked Queenie for helping with the little boy who had cut his hand. "I believe you'd make a good nurse," he said. "You're very composed and steady."

"I'm strong, too," said Queenie, and the doctor smiled.

"Maybe I should hire you," he said as she got out of the car.

It was nearly time for the last bell of the day, and

Little Mother insisted that she felt well enough to go
to her locker by herself. "You'd better see about your
own things," she told Queenie, "if you're planning to
study tonight."

"I can get my books later," said Queenie, and went
with Little Mother to help locate hers.

"I'll need the algebra one and English," said Little
Mother, taking out the two books while Queenie held
open the screen door to the locker. "I've read ahead in
civics and science so I won't take them. And I guess
that's all."

The bell rang and the hall filled immediately with
students hurrying from the building. Dave, Little
Mother's brother, came along and asked, "Are you all
right, Martha? Mr. Hanley told me you had to go to
the doctor." His dark eyes looked more serious than
ever. Queenie used to think his stern expression made
him look mean, but she had changed her mind about
that a long time ago. He looked mature, she had decided.

"I fainted, that was all," answered Little Mother,
and Dave said, "Here, I'll tote your books. And we'd
better hurry or the bus will leave without us."

Little Mother called back over her shoulder, "Bye,
Queenie. And thanks for all you did."

Dave looked back. "So long, Queenie," he said, and
waved at her.

Queenie smiled. "So long," she called to them, thinking Dave looked even nicer than he had in her mind

when she was fitting him and herself into that story she
read at the doctor's office. She felt a little embarrassed
now that she ever had such thoughts. But still, she
wished she knew him better. She bet he worked hard
on the farm. Maybe that gave him the stern expression
she liked, or maybe he got it from his part in managing
that drove of little brothers and sisters. If helping look
after them could cause Little Mother to talk more like
a grownup than a girl, then perhaps it caused Dave to
look a little older around the eyes than he actually was.
She thought more about him and the story she had
read in the magazine while she gathered together the
books she needed.

Starting home, an idea struck her. Dr. Palmer had
said she'd been a help to him and that he should hire
her. She realized he didn't really mean it, but maybe
she could get a part-time job around his office or at the
infirmary doing something. If the bill for Cravey's cast
was to be sent to her and her mother, then maybe she
could work to pay it off. Anyway, she might as well give
it a try, she thought as she turned and walked back
toward town.

Persimmon Gibbs was standing in front of his parents' café when she rounded the corner, but he ran
inside before she got there. She stood in the doorway
and motioned for him to come out, but he sat at the
counter beside his father, who was talking to a cus-
tomer, and pretended not to see. She went ahead
toward Dr. Palmer's office.

The doctor told her he hadn't given any serious thought to part-time help, but that there were times when his staff was overworked by extra chores that came along. Then he smiled. "By the way," he said, "after seeing you all day I still don't know your name."

"It's Queenie Peavy."

The doctor's smile faded. "Queenie Peavy!" he said in a surprised tone. "I didn't realize who you were or expect to find you helping a sick classmate."

"I just helped get her to the first-aid room," said Queenie, "on account of Mr. Page needed somebody. And if you're thinking about the bill for Cravey Mason's broken leg, I promise to work until every last penny of it's paid."

"I wasn't thinking about any bills," said Dr. Palmer. "I was thinking how different you are from what I had pictured Queenie Peavy to be. I heard of the trap you set to cause Cravey's fall and—well—I've heard of various other things you've done, and I suppose I thought you would be a grizzly bear or something."

Queenie got up to leave. "It was just an idea I had, anyway," she said. "I didn't really expect a job."

"It was a good idea," said Dr. Palmer. "We can both think more about it."

Queenie did think about it on the way home, and then she began to wonder: Maybe she wouldn't even be here to accept a job if he offered her one. Maybe she would be far away by then. Cravey kept saying she would be sent to the reformatory; he had even told

everybody at school that his father was going to see to
it. "You're a public nuisance," he had said. "That's what
my pa says."

"A public nuisance," thought Queenie, looking at the
ground as she walked along. "But I didn't break out
those church windows!" A reply came: "No, but you
broke Cravey's leg. And you throw rocks at anybody
who teases you. And you're all the time getting into
fights."

"Not any more," said Queenie. "I've changed."

"Punishment is for what's been done," replied the
voice. "Good intentions should have come earlier."

The voice had an answer for everything, thought
Queenie. She kicked at an empty sardine can on the
edge of the road. "Maybe I really have been a public
nuisance," she said aloud. "Maybe I deserve to be sent
off."

The Shadow of the Jail

The next week Queenie said "I don't care!" anytime her classmates mentioned the reformatory. "I don't care at all!"

Sue Meade told her on Monday during lunch, "I hope you don't have to go. The reformatory is awful-looking. I saw it the last time I was in Atlanta."

"Stop putting on," said Grace Rogers. "You've never been to Atlanta but once."

"That was the last time," said Sue. "And we saw the reformatory. My aunt and uncle pointed it out."

Queenie said, "I don't care."

"It looked lonely," continued Sue. "Ivy was growing up the side of the building and there was nothing else nearby, not even a tree. I'd hate to have to live there."

"I might just like it," said Queenie. "I might just like

it better than this ol' school. And anyway, I don't care!"
It was the same thing she had said over and over to
herself in order not to dwell on thoughts of the likeli-
hood of having to leave home. She was still saying it
as she went into the courthouse that afternoon.

She met the judge on the stairs and he invited her
into his office. When they were seated, she said, "I'm
sorry I acted stupid in the courtroom the other day."

"Yes," said Judge Lewis. "I'm sorry, too."

"And I'm sorry I didn't visit you before now," said
Queenie. There was a brief silence and then she asked,
"Do you still want to see me?"

"I suppose so," said the judge. "I think I want to give
you a lecture." He smiled at her, but she did not say
anything else. "I suppose you've been getting lectures
from 'most everybody, but I'd like to add one more.
You don't mind, do you?" He didn't wait for an answer.
"That was a foolish question, wasn't it? And I'll bet
you're thinking that you couldn't hush me up even if
you did mind, so I'll go ahead with what I want to say."
His voice became softer as he continued. "It never gives
me pleasure to sentence anyone to a penal institution,
but when that person has a child, or children, it hurts
me even more. And even though your father's case was
not tried before me, I'm familiar with the background
of it. And I know it isn't easy for you and your mother
to get by."

"Pa didn't deserve to go to jail," said Queenie. "He
just got mixed up with the wrong crowd, that was all."

"Yes," said the judge, shaking his head. "You're loyal

to your father and that's good. But at the same time, I
must tell you that the wife of one of the other men
insists that her husband was the one who was in bad
company. And do you know what the family of the
third man says? Yes, that he, too, was mixed up with
the wrong crowd." The judge looked at Queenie. "So
you see, when any of us—children, as well as adults—
do things we shouldn't, quite often we, or people close
to us, blame the company we kept instead of ourselves.
And I'm not trying to say that a person can't be dragged
down by associating with sorry companions, but at the
same time each of us is responsible for what we do—
including, certainly, choosing the people we associate
with in the first place. And always we, not they, are
accountable for our own actions. But excuse me, I
didn't mean to preach a sermon."

"I'm paying attention," said Queenie.

"Back to your father," said the judge. "He was sentenced to a prison term, but it was only after he had
been found guilty of his part in the post office robbery.
You do understand, don't you?"

"Yes, sir. I guess so."

"But it occurred to me the other day, after your
defiant behavior in the courtroom, that perhaps you are
living in the shadow of the jail."

"Oh, no, sir," said Queenie. "I live a mile and a half
beyond town off the road to Newnan."

The judge smiled. "I didn't mean where you actually
live. 'The shadow of the jail' is just an expression I've

heard used about people who plain give up in life when
a member of their family is serving time. I've seen it
happen. And sometimes the shadows that are cast are
curious indeed."

Queenie shifted in her chair. "Was that what you
sent for me to tell me?"

"No," said Judge Lewis, "when I sent for you the
other day I had something else in mind. But since then
this other thing has come up."

"What other thing?"

"The sheriff's investigation of your behavior. Since
complaints have been made against you, he's checking
into them thoroughly. I don't know what his conclu-
sions will be, but if the matter is turned over to the
court, tell me what you think we should do about you."

Queenie wanted to say, "Please don't send me away
from home," but she couldn't seem to make herself let
on that she cared. So she crossed her legs and swung
one foot back and forth and said, "I'm not much concerned about it one way or another."

"Reports about you puzzle me," said the judge.
"You've gotten into a lot of trouble in school and
around town, and it's serious when one of your actions
causes a boy's leg to be broken and another results in
destruction of church property." Before Queenie could
say that she hadn't broken those windows, the judge
was saying, "On the other hand, your teachers have
reported that you can be a fine student. It sounds as
if you have a good brain. Don't you think you'd be wise

to use it instead of forever dwelling on your draw-
backs?"

Queenie asked, "What was it you sent for me about
before this ... er ... *this other thing* came up?"

"Well, to be perfectly honest," said Judge Lewis, "I
was trying to do a good deed, but I think I failed. You
see, I'd heard that you're thirteen, and since my own
daughter over at Bridge City is a couple of years older,
I thought perhaps I would bring you some of her things
that might be useful to you." He lowered his voice. "If
you promise not to tell, I'll confess that she's spoiled
terribly. Her mother has always bought her too many
clothes, and not long ago, when they were having a
cleaning-out session, I was shocked at the perfectly
good clothing they were discarding." His eyes twinkled
and he added, "I would have given them a lecture, but
I was afraid my wife would hit me!"

Queenie laughed.

His voice became serious again. "Anyway, it came to
me that I'd ask you to come by and tell me how you're
getting along, and at the same time I could find out if
you'd be offended if I offered you some of the clothes."

"No, sir," said Queenie. "I wouldn't be offended."

"That's a good attitude," said the Judge, "but I hadn't
realized until I walked down the steps with you a few
minutes ago how tall you are. My daughter strikes me
about here." He touched the top pocket of his coat.
"But you're a head taller than that. I hadn't realized
you'd gotten so ... er ..."

"Long-legged?" said Queenie.

The judge laughed. "Gangling, I believe, is the word
I was groping for. And I thank you for coming in to
see me." His tone indicated that the visit was over.

Queenie got up to leave. She wished he would say
something about the reformatory and what would happen if she were believed guilty of all she'd been accused of doing. If he brought up the subject she'd stop
trying to sound as though she didn't care and tell him
that she didn't want to go at all. But he said, "And no
matter what happens, remember that it's up to you not
to let the shadow of the jail cause you to ruin your own
life." She was at the door then and he dismissed her
with, "And I'm sorry about the clothes. But I'm certain
you couldn't begin to get into them."

"That's all right," said Queenie. "I thank you, anyway."

When she was almost home, she met Dover and Avis
along the path. They were taking turns rolling a metal
hoop with a stick and decided to follow her with it.
Dover suggested, "Let's sing some songs."

"No, let's don't," said Queenie. "My mind's too worried."

"That's the time to sing," said Dover. "Didn't you
know that? Come on, Avis, let's sing 'Nobody Knows'
for Queenie."

> "Nobody knows the trouble I've seen,
> Nobody knows my sorrow."

They began at the same time and Queenie joined in on
it. At the end, Dover announced, "Second verse, same

as the first!" as if he were an official song leader, and
started singing again. Their third verse turned out
to be "the same as the first" also, and the song ended
when they arrived at the Peavys' yard.

Queenie flopped down on the back steps. "I may be
leaving here before long," she said.

"How come?" asked Avis, and Dover wanted to know
if Queenie and her mother were moving away.

"Just me," said Queenie. "I might have to go to a
reformatory."

"What's a reformatory?"

"It's a place where they keep bad girls and boys."

Dover said, "But you're not a bad girl."

"Or boy," added Avis.

Queenie told them more about the possibility of her
being sent away and Dover said, "Then you really need
to sing if you've got all those troubles."

"I have to churn," said Queenie, getting up wearily
and starting into the house. "But I reckon I could churn
and listen to you and Avis sing at the same time."

She pulled the churn and a chair out to the top of
the steps and Dover said, "We've decided to dance for
you, too. Maybe that will cheer you up." And he and
Avis began to clap their hands slowly. After they had
settled into a steady rhythm with the clapping, they
shuffled their feet to the same time and a moment later
started to sing the words:

> "Juba this,
> And Juba that,
> And Juba killed the yellow cat."

Gradually, they speeded up until the singing, shuf-
fling, and clapping were at high speed. And Queenie
kept pace with her churning. Soon all three of them
were exhausted and stopped to rest, laughing together.

Queenie looked to see if the butter had gathered, but
the small fluffy bits of cream that had risen to the top
of the milk would not stick to each other. She churned
longer and when the results were still not to her liking
she went inside and brought out a dipperful of warm
water from the stove reservoir and poured a small
amount of it into the vessel. "That ought to speed
things up," she said, starting to churn again while Avis
and Dover, on the bottom step, sang, 'Won't We Have
a Sprightly Time?' Ol' Dominick walked out from behind a cluster of weeds and stood and listened.

After four verses of the song, Queenie looked into
the churn again. "Yep," she said, " 'Won't We Have a
Sprightly Time?' was all it needed! The butter's col-
lected itself together just exactly right." She had just
started into the house to get a bowl when the children's
mother called them from across the pine grove.

"We're coming!" they answered. And Dover, followed by Avis, started along the path, doing a funny,
waddling step, with a kick thrown in every now and
then, that they and Queenie had made up and named
"the gander and the goose promenade."

Queenie took the dasher and lifted the butter into a
bowl of fresh well water. With a small wooden paddle
she began to pat the butter firmly, first from one side
and then another, working the excess milk and air

pockets out of it. When the water in the bowl became cloudy, she poured it off and added a fresh supply. Gradually the fluffy mass of butter changed from a light yellow to a richer shade and a more solid substance. She took it inside then and with the paddle molded it into a cake and set it on a cupboard shelf.

Next, she poured buttermilk from the churn into a big pitcher. In hot weather she would have had to put the buttermilk in a big jar and take it to the spring to stay cool. But other times it kept fresh until the next churning without any special attention. All the same, Queenie wished for an icebox and planned to have one someday. She decided that when she grew up she might just get her one of those electric ones—after she got back from Europe on that three-month honeymoon. That started her thinking about Dave Mullins. He had come over to talk to her in the schoolyard during the morning and had told her that he and his family appreciated her being such a help to Martha last week.

And Little Mother was back in school and feeling fine. She had told Queenie that her father had come into town and got canned beef and things from the welfare office, the way the doctor had suggested. And the farming organization was going to make them a loan. "We're going to get another cow right away," she added excitedly. "The farm office people say we need two cows on account of us being such a big family and milk being so important to health and everything. It's just wonderful the way folks help other folks and

how everything turns out for the best." She had babbled on in her usual way.

Queenie went out to the yard and poured a bucket
of yesterday's buttermilk into a trough for the chickens.
Ol' Dominick got to it first and he began to cluck
loudly. The buff-colored hen and two of the white ones
came running, but the others paid no attention to his
hysterical calling. Queenie laughed. "They don't know
when you're lying and when you're not!" she told him.
She had often seen him stand in the middle of the yard,
hold his beak to the ground as if he had discovered
something delicious to eat, and give his noisy "food-
sharing" call. Then when a few hens gathered around
him he would lift his head and begin to strut and show
off. Sometimes they seemed pleased that he was paying
attention to them and sometimes they did not. Queenie
used to call out, "April fool, you dopey hens!" whenever
she saw any of them gather around Ol' Dominick,
expecting to be fed instead of entertained. She said to
him now, "That's why they don't all believe you when
you're telling the truth." Then she called, "Chick-oop!
Chick-chick-chick-oop!" and the rest of the flock came
running. "See," she said, "they know who to trust!"

She started back toward the house when she saw her
mother walking through the side yard. "Howdy," said
Queenie. "What are you doing home before night?"

"I got off early to come see about a few things here,"
answered Mrs. Peavy. "And I have good news."

"About me?" asked Queenie. "Have they decided to

let me stay home instead of being sent off?" She smiled as if she were certain this would be the good news.

But her smile disappeared when her mother answered, "No, it's not about that."

"Then what is it?" asked Queenie, disgustedly.

"Your pa's coming home."

Queenie yelled, "Whoopee! Is he really? When? When's he coming?"

"Tomorrow."

"Tomorrow!" said Queenie, turning around and around and whirling the empty buttermilk bucket in circles over her head. When she was dizzy, she leaned against the well for support. "Tomorrow!" she said again. "That's the grandest thing that ever happened!"

Her mother said sadly, "But I have bad news, too. The sheriff told me today that he has almost finished his investigation. And according to him, evidence is strong against you—with Persimmon swearing he saw you break those church windows and the preacher's wife and different ones recalling that you were throwing rocks at everything you saw that day. The way he talked, lots of folks are saying that if I can't make you behave decent then you ought to be turned over to authorities who can. Only I don't——"

She started to say more, but Queenie interrupted her. "Oh, Ma," she said, "they'll change their mind, you know they will. They've got to!"

"Why have they got to?"

"On account of Pa coming home," said Queenie.

"We've waited so long, and besides they'll know I'll behave just fine from now on. They'll know that most of my trouble has been brought on by folks aggravating me 'cause Pa was in jail and that if he's not there anymore they won't need to worry about me one little bit. My problems are over just like that!" She snapped her fingers to show how quickly her situation had improved.

All her mother said was: "I hope you're right."

The Pride of the County

The next afternoon Queenie didn't try to catch Persimmon the way she had been doing. She decided not to risk making matters worse by getting into another scrap. She was still hurt that he had done her such a mean turn, but it was not nearly so important to her now. The thing that mattered was that her father had been paroled, and she hurried home to see him.

Her mother had taken half a day off from the canning plant, and was with her father in the house. They were sitting in her mother's room—only from now on it would be her father's room, too.

"Pa!" cried Queenie excitedly. "You're home!" She ran over to the rocking chair where he sat, planning to kiss him. But he did not reach out to her and she stopped

abruptly and stood in front of him. She didn't know
what to say next, so she said again, "You're home." This
time she said it as if she couldn't quite believe it.

"Yes, I'm home," said her father, smiling at her.

"I'm glad you are," said Queenie. "I sure am glad you
are."

"Me, too," said her father. "Anything beats the penitentiary." He got to his feet, and she thought maybe he
was going to put his arms around her. Maybe he had
been so overcome by seeing her again that he'd been
too happy to know what to do at first. But he started
toward the kitchen. "I'm thirsty," he said. "Is the bucket
still in the same place?"

"I'll get you a dipperful," said Queenie, hurrying to
bring him the gourd filled with water.

When he took it, he noticed his daughter's height and
said, "You get lankier and lankier, don't you, String
Bean?"

Queenie laughed. "I sure do, Pa. Lankier and lankier."

"She's getting prettier," said her mother, while Mr.
Peavy drank the water. "Why can't you tell her that?"

Her father handed back the dipper. "Cain't tell her
anything I ain't noticed," he said, slapping Queenie on
the back. Both of them laughed, but her mother did
not. Her father continued, "Go do your night work,
Queenie. We're gonna eat supper early and go into
town."

"Are we really?" asked Queenie.

"Just your ma and me. We got to see some folks."

Queenie's smile disappeared as she started out. "Don't you want to come with me and see how the chickens are looking and all?"

"Cain't say that I do," said her father, sitting back in the rocker.

Queenie left, but she was sorry to be urged out of the house. She wanted to talk with her father—and just get to look at him for a while, too. And besides, it was early for doing the chores. She told Ol' Dominick, after she had fed the chickens, "You think I'm going crazy, don't you?—doing the night work ahead of time. And unless you tell 'em better, those dumb hens will be so confused they'll decide it's time to go to roost." He flew onto the post that held the clothesline, flapped his wings, and crowed. Queenie reached up and patted him. "Tell 'em again!" she said, and he crowed once more as she walked away.

Sweetheart was not at the gate or anywhere in sight, and Queenie walked down into the pasture. She brooded over being sent from the house until she thought of the most likely reason her father and mother were going into town. She guessed they would call on Sheriff Townsend and Deputy Ellins, and Judge Lewis, if they got there before he left his office, and maybe Cravey Mason's father, too, since it seemed that he was one of the main ones agitating for something to be done about her. She imagined her father was going to ask everybody to leave his daughter alone. He would assure them that his girl would be so good, now that he was home, that everyone in these parts would be proud of her. Queenie Peavy would be the pride of the county.

That's what she was thinking when she finally located Sweetheart on the far side of the pasture, eating kudzu through the barbed-wire fence. Amaryllis was there, too, and Queenie drove both cows to the barn. By the time she got there it was almost the usual milking time.

Elgin Corry came along soon, followed by Dover, Avis, and Matilda. Avis and Dover swung on the door of one of the stables and Matilda sat and watched them. Elgin said, "Children, don't make me have to tell you again that you're too heavy for such as that. You'll ruin the hinges." They went into another part of the barn and a few moments later the squeaking sounds of the feed-room door opening and closing indicated that they were swinging on it. But Elgin did not call to them. Instead, he told Queenie, "I hate to stay on 'em all the time. I can remember when I was their age it came natural to always be swinging on anything that would move."

Queenie got up from her milking stool to pour a pan of milk into the bucket. When she sat down again, she said, "Pa's home. Did you know that?"

"I heard he was coming. How's he getting along?"

"He's fine," she answered cheerily. "He sure is glad to get home and see me and Mamma again."

She waited for Elgin to say how pleased he was to hear the news; but instead he called to Avis and Dover, "Come here a minute, I want to talk to you." They came over and stood near him and he continued, "Queenie tells me that Mr. Peavy is home."

"Yes, sir," said Avis. "We heard. We were sitting over there in the feed room all the time."

Elgin laughed. "You were swinging on the feed-room door, you mean. But that's not why I called you. I want to remind you that you're not to be playing near Queenie's house any more. Do you hear me?"

"How come?" asked Dover.

" 'Cause I said not to," answered Elgin sternly. "And 'cause Mr. Peavy might not like it if you yell and holler and carry on with a lot of noise. His nerves may not be too good after all he's been through and——"

Queenie interrupted. "Oh, Pa's nerves are just fine. And if you suspect he's apt to get mad and chase Dover and Avis off, I'm sure he won't. Oh, I know some folks claim Pa's got a mean streak, but they don't know him, that's all."

Someone in the doorway of the barn said, "You tell 'em, String Bean!" and Queenie looked up to see her father coming inside. He spoke to Elgin, who had got up to turn Amaryllis into the lot.

"Howdy," greeted Elgin.

Queenie's father asked, "How's it going?"

"Fine, I reckon. Glad to see you back."

Dover and Avis began edging away, but Elgin stopped them. "Children," he said, "say 'hello' to Mr. Peavy."

Dover said, "Howdy-do, Mr. Peavy," but bashfulness

suddenly came on Avis and she looked down at the
ground and would not lift her head.

Queenie said, "They've grown a heap since you saw
them, haven't they, Pa?"

"Not as much as you," he said pleasantly. "But I came
to tell you that your ma and I are leaving for town."

"But what about your supper?"

"After you were so long getting back, we went ahead
and ate."

"I had to hunt for Sweetheart," explained Queenie as
her father left the stable.

He called back to her, "Your supper's on the stove."

Queenie felt cheated. Here he was home and she had
barely seen or talked to him. She reminded herself,
however, that it was probably on her account that he
was so anxious to go into town. He must not be able to
wait another minute to get started. She called after him,
"Bye, Pa. Have a good time in town!" But if he heard
her he did not turn around to answer.

Queenie ate supper by herself and then put away the
dishes from the kitchen table and brought out her
books. She planned to excel in her school work tomorrow. And she would behave so well, too, that everybody
would see right off the change that had come over her
the minute her father got home. Nobody was apt to say
anything that would make her mad, she knew, since the
remarks that unloosed her temper always had to do
with her father's being in prison. Now that he was

home, nobody could irritate her about it. But even if they could, she decided, she wouldn't let it upset her—because she was going to improve so drastically. She intended to astound everyone: Queenie Peavy would definitely be the pride of the county!

She studied her algebra problems for the next day, reworking each one until she understood it clearly, and then stopped to think more about her own situation. She wondered where her parents were at that moment. Had they seen Sheriff Townsend already? Had they arrived in town before Judge Lewis left? What about Cravey's father? She bet they would talk sense into everybody before the night was over, and she wouldn't any more have to go off to that ol' reformatory than a jack rabbit.

She got out her notebook and began writing sentences for English homework. "My rooster's name is Ol' Dominick," she wrote first. It showed the apostrophe being used to denote possession in one instance and to take the place of an omitted letter in another. "Well, how about that!" she said to herself, pleased that she had come across the second example accidentally.

Next, she began to read her science book. She read beyond the pages assigned for the lesson because she was not sleepy—and, too, she wanted to stay awake until her parents came home.

After a while she had studied her lessons until she was well prepared in all of them. But her mother and father were not home yet and she began to wonder what was taking them such a long time. She left her English book open on the table in front of her, and whenever she heard any kind of noise outside, she would bend over the book and appear to be reading it, deep in concentration. She wanted her parents to think she was sitting up late because she still had homework to do instead of because she was curious to find out what had happened in town. But the noises outside always turned out to be false alarms, twigs breaking or perhaps animals from the woods scurrying about, not the return of Mr. and Mrs. Peavy.

At first she was not sleepy, but gradually she began to nod. Then suddenly there was a crackling noise on the dried leaves near the side of the house and she was wide awake once more. She bent over the English book and waited.

Several minutes passed and nothing happened. Then she heard the crackling noise again and could not pretend to study any longer. She ran to the door and opened it. "Ma?" she called into the yard. "Pa? Are you there?"

No answer came and then she saw the Corrys' hound standing near the steps. "Aw, Matilda!" she said dejectedly, "was that you crunching around out there?" and went back inside.

She gave up then, and got into bed. It was so long past her usual bedtime that she went to sleep almost by the time she pulled the cover under her chin.

During the night she heard, or thought she heard, her

mother and father coming into the house, but she was too sleepy to rouse herself to say anything. Soon she drifted back to sleep, thinking she was overhearing them talk. Such phrases as "out of your mind drinking even one drop of whisky when you're on parole" and "no firearms" came from her mother. Her father's voice, sounding gruff, was low. He seemed to be telling his wife that he wished she would not nag at him on his first day home.

In the morning, Queenie overslept. She usually woke up the moment daylight came into the room, but this time the sun had cleared the horizon before she knew it had even begun to rise. She dressed quickly, got a fire started in the cookstove, and then hurried to the barn to do the milking—after tiptoeing into the next room and waking her mother.

It was a beautiful morning, and she felt refreshed and good until the thoughts came back to her about the conversations in the night. Then she decided she hadn't really heard them. She must have only dreamed them, the way she sometimes did when she was too anxious about anything.

Smoke was coming out of the chimney at Elgin Corry's house and Queenie could smell ham cooking. Nothing smelled quite as good on a crisp, clear morning. Elgin was leaving the barn when Queenie got to it. "Good morning," he said. "Sun-up comes early, don't it?"

Queenie smiled. "I thought I was later than I am."
She was relieved to find that he wasn't too far ahead of
her with his work. She bet he never overslept.

When she got home with the milk, her mother was in
the kitchen. The fire was roaring hot now, and fatback
and eggs were frying on top of the stove while biscuits
from the day before were being warmed in the oven.
Only two plates were on the table, and Queenie
laughed. "You forgot to set a place for Pa!"

"He's still sleeping," answered Mrs. Peavy. "We'd
better not wake him this time." She put the breakfast
on the table and the two of them sat down.

Talking softly, so as not to wake her father, Queenie
asked, "What did you find out last night?"

"About what?"

"About me. Is anybody still saying I need to be sent
off? Wasn't that what you and Pa went to town about?"

Mrs. Peavy looked up. "No," she said. "That wasn't it.
Your father wanted to see a few old friends. And you
may just as well know it, he also wanted to see a few old
enemies—ones he thinks should have lied in court to
keep him out of jail." She broke the yellow of a fried
egg and sopped at it with a biscuit. Then she continued
the conversation. "But I've been trying all along to persuade the sheriff that the charges against you ought to
be dropped. I had hoped to convince him that you'd do
all right from now on."

"Did you sway him? Can't he see what a good effect
Pa's being home will have on me?"

Her mother shook her head. "If your father obeys his parole officer and goes by the rules, it will help all of us in the long run. Of course, your behavior will count, too." She added slowly, "And I just as well . . ." She stopped there, as if she dreaded to say more. "Have some butter and pass it to me," she said briskly. "Let's finish breakfast."

Queenie ate in silence and then began getting ready for school. "I left my civics book on a chair in yonder," she said, motioning toward the other room.

"Tiptoe in and get it," said Mrs. Peavy, putting pieces of the fatback between biscuits for a lunch for Queenie and one for herself to take to the canning plant.

Queenie entered the other room quietly. Her father turned over in the bed as if he might be awake, but soon he was breathing heavily and she knew he was still asleep. She eased over to the corner where she had left the book. Her father's work jacket was hung on the back of the chair, and she reached over it and lifted the book without making a sound. But suddenly she saw something that made her gasp. She straightened up and stood motionless.

A second later she looked over at her father, but he had not awakened. Her gaze then returned to what had startled her. The sun shone in through the window and she saw clearly that she had not been mistaken. Sticking out of the jacket pocket was the handle of a pistol.

Queenie backed away from it—as if it were a snake or a wild animal that might not strike if she managed to back out of range without attracting its attention. At the door, she turned and hurried to the kitchen table.

"Ma!" she said, sitting down in one of the chairs.

"Here's your lunch," said Mrs. Peavy. "And your father's breakfast is in the warming closet. I'd better be on my way."

"Ma," said Queenie, "we better do all we can to help Pa not break any of his parole rules or anything."

"Yes, we'd better," agreed her mother, wrapping a piece of newspaper around her own lunch. "And before I leave, there's something else . . ." She hesitated, then started over. "I've been trying to tell you—the sheriff says his investigation of you proves there'll have to be a trial or a court hearing or something."

Queenie looked as if she had been slapped. Her eyes widened and her mouth dropped open and she put her hands to her head. She said nothing for a few seconds. Then she asked, "Will they put me in jail?"

"No," answered Mrs. Peavy. "I signed an appearance bond, which means I promised them you won't run away and that you'll appear at the hearing or the trial, whichever they decide to have."

"Listen to the Mockingbird"

Working hours at the canning plant began at seven o'clock in the morning, and school did not start until after eight. Mrs. Peavy always left home more than an hour ahead of Queenie, who used the extra time for chores.

The first morning her father was home she carried two armloads of stovewood into the house, dumping them as quietly as possible into the box by the stove. She listened to see if there was any stirring from the direction of the next room, but all was quiet. She then took the bucket from the washstand and went to the well, filled the bucket with fresh water, and returned to the kitchen. When she was easing the bucket back into its accustomed place, the side of it scraped against the rim of the washpan with a slight screech. And when she turned loose the handle of the bucket it fell to the side with a clinking noise.

Queenie tiptoed from the room and went through the woods to the barn. Sweetheart and Amaryllis had finished their morning rations and stood at the door. "I'll take both cows to the pasture," she called across the lot to Elgin, who was nailing scraps of lumber together to make a fattening pen for his hogs.

When she returned to the house, she found Mr. Peavy at the kitchen table, eating his breakfast. "Howdy, Pa," said Queenie. "I thought maybe you wanted to sleep late."

"I did want to."

"This being your first morning home and all, I figured you'd——"

Her father interrupted. "How could anybody sleep with all the blamming going on?"

"I didn't mean to make so much fuss when I brought in the water a while ago," she said, smiling at him. "I just can't seem to help it: Whenever I try to be quiet something always goes wrong."

"It's okay," said Mr. Peavy. "I needed to get up."

"I'm not going to school today," announced Queenie, as the thought came to her. "I'm not supposed to stay out, of course, but I'm in so much trouble already that one more thing won't make any difference."

Her father smiled. "You've got the right idea," he said. "Don't let anybody push you around!"

That made Queenie feel better. "Maybe you can help me think of a way to get out of the mess I'm in," she said. "You'll probably know exactly what to do."

Mr. Peavy stopped eating. "Where's the pepper?" he asked. "Eggs need pepper; your ma ought to know that."

"Oh, we don't have any pepper," said Queenie. "It's one of the things we don't just have to have, but maybe we'll buy a supply of it—now that you're home." She hopped up and went to the cupboard. "But we've got lots of salt," she said proudly, bringing out a box of it. "Wouldn't you like some more salt? Maybe it would help the eggs."

"They're too salty already," he said, and Queenie sat back down. She didn't know what to say next. If her father didn't want to hear about her, maybe she ought to talk about him; maybe she should let him know that she was interested in whatever he cared to discuss. She would show him right off that he could talk about anything with her. After all, she was his daughter.

She tried once more. "I sure am glad you're home, Pa."

"You said that yesterday."

"I know," said Queenie, laughing. "But it's so good to have you here I feel like saying it over and over." Her father did not smile and she stopped laughing and looked him square in the eyes. After a few seconds she asked, "What was it like? Tell me what it was like . . ." She started to say "in the penitentiary," but it wouldn't quite come out, and she began again. "What was it like up in Atlanta?"

"I'm going to town," said Mr. Peavy, getting out of his chair.

"I'll go with you."

"Go to school or stay home," he said.

"I'll go to school," said Queenie, hurrying to get her books. "We can go that far together."

Along the trail, her father walked fast and she had to run to keep up with him. "Let's slow down," she suggested when they arrived at the main road. She was not tired, but maybe if they walked slower they would talk. But a sawmill truck came along, and her father put out his right thumb for a lift. The truck stopped, and he sprang onto one of the logs it was hauling.

Queenie said, "I never have flagged down a truck or anything."

"Girls ain't supposed to," said Mr. Peavy.

She held out her books to him, thinking he would hold them while she climbed aboard, but instead he called loudly to the driver, "I'm on! Take off!" The truck pulled away and Queenie had to jump back so quickly to avoid being hit by the logs that she fell backward into a ditch.

She sat there while the truck drove out of sight, then got up slowly, brushed herself off, and walked in the direction of town. She considered skipping school. She figured it was only a matter of time now before she would be sent to a reformatory, anyway, and that this was the last day she would be expected to attend school in Cotton Junction. She imagined that Mr. Hanley would call her into his office before the end of the day and tell her to clean out her locker and go on home. He'd probably say how sorry he was, but that anybody about to have a court trial or hearing had to be kicked out of school. He would say it in a nicer way, but that's what he would mean. Well, she might not be there to hear him, she decided; she would just do whatever she pleased today.

A year earlier she would have gone with Floyd Speer and Persimmon, or anybody she could find, and hidden out with them at the city dump. They would have divided their time between laughing about stealing the holiday and throwing rocks at tin cans and other rubbish. The city dump was full of ideal targets. But that was last year.

Today she didn't want to play hooky or influence anyone else to become a truant. She decided there was nothing she would rather do than go to school. There was to be a laboratory session in science that ought to be downright interesting. And the debate in civics class from yesterday was being continued. She still couldn't get over how much fun debating was. It was better than a good fight, she had decided, or maybe it *was* a good fight—an organized one with words as the ammunition. And she and Sue Meade might just win. They had put up a good argument: *Resolved, That governors of this state should be elected for four years instead of two.* A boys' team was arguing that the two-year term should not be changed, and Mr. Page was judging. And besides

all that, this was assembly day and the eighth grade was
in charge of the program.

It was to have been such a good day. She remembered how she'd planned last night to settle down and
cooperate with everybody and be pleasant and work
hard to get along well. When she thought of it, she
smiled as if she were thinking of someone else, a girl
who had thought she could suddenly turn from one
thing into another. "You're a far sight from being the
pride of the county!" she said to herself. "You're nothing
but a gawky troublemaker headed for the reformatory."

Then a thought occurred to her: I could still show
up at school acting as if a big change had come over me.
I could cooperate and be considerate of everybody and
all. It might keep me from dwelling on the fact that this
is probably my last day, and it would be a good joke on
everybody else. They'll wonder what's got into me. She
felt better and began to sing "Listen to the Mockingbird," but she stopped abruptly. "Aw, what's the use?
I can't be happy when I'm not."

But all the resolutions of the night before kept coming back to her. They had made such good sense, and
now they were lining themselves up in her mind, refus-
ing to be ignored. "It must be all that debating I've
been doing," she said. "Very well, I'll behave myself this
whole day. And nothing will stop me! I'll be a mockingbird and pretend that I'm something I'm not." Sounding
more determined than happy, she began to sing again
and did not stop until she arrived at school.

The second bell for homeroom period had not rung

when she got there and her classmates were at their desks, chatting. Little Mother said, "Miss Collins was in here a few minutes ago. She says that instead of spelling this morning we're going to discuss a class wiener roast."

"Good!" said Queenie, remembering her decision to appear pleasant all day. "I'm really looking forward to our wiener roast. Yes siree!"

When the bell rang Miss Collins came back into the room. "Instead of all of us trying to plan our outing," she said, "I think it might be best if we elected a social committee and let its members work out the details."

Everybody agreed: Yes, that was the only way to have a party. And Queenie decided she would nominate herself as chairman. That would give the whole crowd a laugh. And she could imagine Miss Collins saying, "Now, dear, I don't really think it's the thing to do for one to nominate oneself." She smiled at the thought, then listened again to what was being said. Miss Collins was asking if anyone cared to suggest someone as head of the social committee. Queenie's hand flew up.

"Yes?" said Miss Collins.

Queenie got to her feet. "I nominate . . . er . . . I nominate . . ." She hesitated.

"Yes, go ahead, dear."

Queenie started over. "I nominate Cravey Mason," she said, and sat down.

The room suddenly became still. In elections, the students usually nominated their good friends. Maybe for class president or vice president or something like

that, qualifications would be considered. But on anything as important as a social committee chairman, a
person would propose a friend for certain. The entire
class seemed stunned at Queenie's nominating Cravey,
her archenemy. At last the silence was broken when
Kate Coogler said, "I second the motion."

"It wasn't a motion, silly," said Grace Rogers, "but a
nomination."

"Then I second the nomination," said Kate. Melvin
McWhorter said he didn't think a nomination had to be
seconded, and an argument got under way.

"Students!" called Miss Collins. Everyone quieted
down and she told them, "Remember, keep our voices
low or we'll go back to the spelling lesson." Then she
asked if there were other nominations for chairman.
There were none and Cravey was elected by a show of
hands.

Miss Collins said then she would appoint the committee members, but the class wanted to do more elect-
ing and she allowed them to nominate candidates. Four
girls and three boys had been proposed by the time the
bell rang. No time was left to vote and Miss Collins
said, "All seven of you may serve as Cravey's committee. And our meeting stands adjourned. Hurry, everyone, to your next class!"

On the way Little Mother said to Queenie, "Wasn't
that a lovely election? Everybody who was nominated
was elected and I think that's the way it ought to be. I
do so hate ever to vote against a person, and even

though I realize I should look at it as if I'm voting *for* somebody, not *against* anyone, it still seems awfully pleasant when nobody loses." She chattered on until they got to English class about what a lovely election it had been and how pleased she was that Queenie had nominated Cravey as chairman. "I'm glad you don't bear malice," she concluded as Mrs. Thaxton walked into the room.

Queenie smiled over at Little Mother, as if she really had nominated Cravey because she felt friendly toward him. She thought about what a good act she was putting on and smiled again.

Mrs. Thaxton asked, "What's so funny, Queenie?"

"Ma'am?"

"What's so funny? You were sitting there smiling."

"Oh . . . er . . . I don't know. 'Cause I know my lesson, I guess."

"Let's see if you do," she said. "We'll skip to the diagraming portion of it and you may do sentence eleven for us."

Queenie went to the blackboard and quickly wrote out the sentence, "When we have prepared our lessons, we do better work because we understand the principles of diagraming," showing that *we do better work* was an independent clause and the *when* and *because* ones were dependent and adverbial.

"Very good indeed!" said Mrs. Thaxton. "And I'll smile, too, if the rest of the class will do as well."

At the end of the period, Miss Collins stopped

Queenie in the hall. "Our room is in charge of the assembly program this afternoon," she said, "and Jane Coleman and Nettie Brock were to sing a duet, but Jane is absent today and Nettie refuses to sing by herself or with anyone else. I'm wondering if you would sing a solo for us."

Queenie was about to say "Not this time" when she remembered that this was her day to be a completely new person. "Why, yes, ma'am," she answered. "I'll be happy to sing a song."

Miss Collins appeared shocked. She had asked Queenie before to take part in programs but had always been turned down. "Mrs. Bray will help you pick out something and will accompany you on the piano. Could you meet her in the auditorium at noon?"

"Yes, ma'am," said Queenie. "I'll be happy to." And she hurried ahead to study hall, leaving Miss Collins with a puzzled look on her face.

Mrs. Bray was waiting in the auditorium when the bell rang at twelve o'clock and they tried two songs—a ballad, "Past Midnight the Nightingale Sang of My Home," and a funny one called "Sudie Had a Suitor."

"You do them both so well," said Mrs. Bray. "I don't know which one we should select. Maybe the nightingale one, if that suits you?"

"Yes, ma'am," said Queenie, starting to leave, "it suits me fine."

When she got back to the homeroom everyone had gone outside except Little Mother, who, after hearing

about the song for the assembly program, began chatter-
ing about how lovely it must be to have a nice singing
voice and how generous it was to use a talent to give
pleasure to others. As always, she sounded more like a
grownup than a girl. Then she said, "In honor of the
program, why don't you pin your hair back? I'll bet
you'd look fetching if you kept it out of your eyes."

"I like it straggly," said Queenie.

"Oh, I didn't mean it looked straggly," insisted Little
Mother. "But it might just be especially pretty pushed
back." She said it so many more times that Queenie
finally gave in, when she had eaten her lunch. Little
Mother lent her the two bobby pins from her own hair.
"Mine will likely stay back of its own accord," she said.
"And anyway, I'm not to sing in front of the whole
school."

That gave Queenie an uneasy feeling, and she might
have changed her mind if lunch period hadn't ended at
that moment. Classmates began returning to their
places to be ready to march into the auditorium at the
next bell.

Miss Collins announced that everyone on the program was to hurry ahead to the stage. Queenie flopped
down in her desk. She believed she wouldn't sing after
all. If anybody didn't like it, what did it matter? What
could they do to her that was any worse than being sent
to a reformatory?

"Queenie, dear," said Miss Collins. "Didn't you hear
me? Those of you on the program should hurry to the
auditorium."

Almost to the High Ground

She started to tell Miss Collins that she wasn't going to sing. Then she remembered that she wanted everybody to think she had reformed before she even went to the reformatory. She was cooperating for herself. Springing out of her seat, she said, "Yes, ma'am, I'll hurry."

Mrs. Bray smiled at her when she took her place in the row of chairs on the stage. "You look sweet with more of your face showing." Queenie had almost forgotten her new hair style.

The student body marched in then, and Mr. Hanley made the announcements. When he was finished, he turned the program over to the eighth grade. First there was a reading by Margaret Elton, one of the girls who lived in town. It was entitled "Connie and I Were Go-

ing to the Morning Service," and was all about two
women who set out to church in a buggy pulled by a
stubborn mule. And when they came to a railroad crossing, the mule stopped on the rails and refused to move
off—even though a train was coming! Margaret Elton
took elocution lessons after school one day a week and
was an expert reader.

After that, Melvin McWhorter and two other boys
stood up. Each one of them said a short piece about the
importance of being a good citizen and how everybody
should be concerned with government. At the end, all
three of them said together: "It's everybody's business."

Queenie's song was supposed to be next and she
stood up when Mrs. Bray began the piece on the piano.
But she felt dizzy all of a sudden. Her legs seemed
ready to give way and her stomach had the most awful,
empty feeling. She wished she had never gotten into
this predicament and tried to remember why she had
ever thought it was a good idea. "My day to pretend . . ." she said to herself. "Pretend nobody's listening . . . pretend you're on the backsteps and only Ol'
Dominick is within hearing distance."

The piano stopped and Mrs. Bray cleared her throat.
Queenie had missed her starting place. A few people
in the audience snickered when the accompaniment
started over.

This time Queenie began at the proper place and on
exactly the right pitch. In her clear contralto voice she
began the first verse of "Past Midnight the Nightingale

Sang of My Home." A slight tremble was in her voice, but it disappeared as she began to think about what the words meant. When she got to the part about the person in the song being run away from home, she almost sobbed—which was precisely the spot that should have sounded especially sad. Imagining that she sang to Ol' Dominick only, with woods and fields surrounding them, she sang out the last two verses with genuine feeling.

The audience applauded until Mr. Hanley stood up. "That was a rare treat for us," he said. "We could stay to hear another number if our musicians have one ready."

"We have an encore," said Mrs. Bray, beginning to play "Sudie Had a Suitor" without giving Queenie a chance to protest.

The trouble with Sudie was that she had a suitor at the front door and one on the back porch at the same time, and she was kept busy running back and forth between the two. Queenie sang this time for the audience. They had been nice to clap the way they did, and she would just sing for them instead of pretending it was for Ol' Dominick only. And the audience responded by laughing and cheering wildly when she finished.

Mr. Hanley stood up, laughing also. "We have to go back to classes now," he said, "but let's get Queenie to take a final bow." At that, he and everyone else cheered until Queenie stood up and bowed.

"A final bow," she thought, wondering when she

would ever see inside this auditorium and schoolhouse
after today.

Miss Collins patted her on the back as she came off
the stage. "It was just beautiful, dear," she said. "Why,
when you got to the sad part in the first song, I just
thought I would cry."

Queenie smiled. "Me, too," she said.

On the way home Queenie worried. She had expected
all day to be called into Mr. Hanley's office and told not
to come back to school any more. But he hadn't sent for
her. She was still wondering about it as she made her
way through the swamps near the Corrys' place.

Almost to the high ground, she met her father coming
along the trail. "Howdy, Pa," she said. "I didn't know
you'd be back this early."

"I've been around a while," he answered, "but I'm
headed to town again."

Queenie said, "Then it appears you and I are going
opposite directions." She gave him time to invite her to
turn and go back with him. Instead, he asked if she had
been hurt when she jumped back from the sawmill
truck.

Queenie smiled. "Shucks, no, Pa. A little thing like
that wouldn't hurt me." She lifted an elbow to show
him the long scratches on it. "I wasn't even bruised but
just a little bit, and I didn't expect you to stop the truck
and come back to see about me." She hadn't meant to

say that. Now he would know that she had felt let down
when he had ridden away without appearing to be concerned about her. Quickly she added, "It just scared me
a little, that was all."

"Let it be a lesson to you," said Mr. Peavy. "Don't
ever ride with anybody you don't know."

"I won't, Pa," she promised, and as he started away,
she caught a glimpse of the pistol handle in the pocket
of his jacket. "Wait, Pa!" she called.

"What for?" he asked impatiently.

"I know it's not any of my business," she said, trying
not to sound alarmed, "but I can't help noticing that
you have a pistol with you. Maybe you forgot to leave
it at home?" She reached out her hand. "Would you like
for me to take it back for you?"

"You're right!" he said, and Queenie felt pleased.
"You're absolutely right," he added, "it's none of your
business!" With that, he walked away, leaving her more
stunned than when she had fallen backwards into the
ditch.

She sat down on a tree stump and watched him dis-
appear. If only he wouldn't tote a gun. Wasn't he going
to make any effort to abide by parole rules, and didn't
he care anything about her or her mother? She wondered suddenly if he cared about anybody besides himself. It hurt even to think in such a way.

Other thoughts came into her mind. She remembered
fights she had got into over the years, arguments she'd
had and stones she had thrown, and realized it was her

fierce loyalty to her father that had kept getting her into difficulty—loyalty to him and resentment against almost everyone else. Yet she had known all the time, and refused to face up to it, that he had brought on his own troubles. She knew nobody had picked on him and that she must learn to be honest with herself. Otherwise she would grow into a bitter, suspicious person who would always think the world and everybody in it was against her. Her father had been imprisoned because he was found guilty of committing a crime. Laws were made to be obeyed; what if everybody broke them?

She thought also of the difference between him and the man she had planned for him to be—the one she had built up in her imagination. Maybe she had expected too much, maybe she was being unfair. But, having him home again had seemed the most important thing in the world to her. Wasn't it important to him? And didn't he even care that she might be sent off to a reformatory?

She blinked to hold back a tear, but it ran down her cheek anyway. It was followed by another one—and another. Soon she was weeping in spite of herself, and she wondered if she were going crazy. She never had broken down like this.

She was still sniffing when someone behind her said softly, "Don't cry." She jumped up to run, thinking she was hearing the "swamp voices" that other people claimed to have heard on occasion.

"Dover and Avis!" she said, turning around. "I didn't see you come along the trail."

Dover pointed behind them. "We came from over there. We were picking up acorns for the hogs."

"I'm sorry you caught me crying," said Queenie. "I don't know what came over me."

Avis confided, "I cry sometimes."

"I don't," said Queenie, sitting down on the stump again. "It's not my policy."

Matilda strolled out from the underbrush, and Dover said, "Ask Matilda how things are going in the tree-tops."

"I know," replied Queenie, brushing away one last tear. "She helped me gather hickory nuts the other day."

"Aw, she didn't either!" whined Avis.

"Did she really?" asked Dover, winking.

"Climbed the tree and shook every limb," said Queenie, pointing toward a giant hickory. "I wish Avis could have seen her hop from branch to branch."

"Aw, you're making that up!" insisted Avis. At the same time, she stared at the tree as if she could almost visualize Matilda in the top of it.

"Matilda's a good hopper," said Dover. "That's on account of she's part rabbit."

Avis insisted that last time it had been *part fox,* and before that, *part bobcat,* and that she didn't really believe all those stories.

While they argued, it occurred to Queenie that her own views of her father might be akin to the notions

Avis held of Matilda. Avis wanted to accept made-up stories as the truth, but she surely knew that the dog was no more than an ordinary hound. And to Queenie, Mr. Peavy was not the hero she wished him to be. She must not lie to herself about that or anything else. She loved him still, but she would never again pretend anything was true that wasn't. She put one arm around Avis, who was losing the argument with Dover, and said, "You've known all the time, haven't you? *Potliquor hounds can't climb trees.*"

A Stone's Throw

Mrs. Peavy arrived home by sundown that evening, but Mr. Peavy did not get there until far into the night. He was still asleep the next morning, and Queenie did the chores as quietly as possible. When the work was finished, she left for school—certain that this would be the day she would be told to leave.

But nothing out of the ordinary happened until algebra class in the afternoon. Mary Nolan knocked at the door and said that Cravey Mason was wanted in Mr. Hanley's office. Toward the end of the period Mary brought a message that Queenie Peavy was wanted in the office, too.

Queenie started down the hall. She supposed Mr. Hanley wanted to tell her to turn back any school property, library books and things, before she left at the end of the day. Well, he needn't worry that she would try to steal anything. She would give back every book before she left.

Mr. Hanley called, "Come in," when she arrived at his office door.

Inside, Queenie saw that not only was Cravey there, but Persimmon had been called over from the grammar school.

"Have a seat," said Mr. Hanley, and after Queenie sat down he continued. "I believe you will be pleased to hear part of what I have to say and saddened by part of it. The good news first: you've been cleared of the charges of breaking those church windows."

"Have I really?" asked Queenie, excitedly. "Who cleared me?"

"Persimmon here," said Mr. Hanley, "whose story has been corroborated by Cravey."

"Well, good for you, Persimmon! And thank you, too, Cravey." Then Queenie turned back to Mr. Hanley and asked, "What was it that was going to sadden me?"

Mr. Hanley said, "The fact that your friend Persimmon broke those windows himself. And, also, that he was put up to it, even bribed to do it and blame you, by Cravey."

Queenie started to say, "Why, that doesn't sadden me a bit," but then she thought, yes, it did, too. Even though she had suspected all along what had actually happened, it did hurt to know for certain that anyone would do such a thing. "I'm sorry to hear about it," she told Mr. Hanley. "Do Cravey and Persimmon get to go to the reformatory now instead of me?"

Mr. Hanley smiled. "You're a hard one to figure out. You hadn't been sentenced to any reformatory except in your own mind. But you sound almost as if you were looking forward to going there."

"Oh, no, sir," said Queenie.

"The charges against you have been dismissed," continued Mr. Hanley. "After I got the truth out of Persimmon, he and I went to the sheriff and explained things. I doubt that anybody will be sent to the reformatory, but the boys will have to earn enough money to replace those windows."

"I'll help 'em out," said Queenie. "If they were good enough to come forward and tell the truth, then I'll just pitch in and help them earn some money." She didn't add that it would have to be after she had paid the doctor for Cravey's cast.

"I don't expect they'll let you help pay for the windows," said Mr. Hanley. Looking at the boys, he added sternly, "Will you?"

Cravey said meekly, "No, sir."

"And why not?" asked Mr. Hanley, looking directly at Persimmon.

Persimmon hung his head and squirmed in his chair. "Because we didn't come forward with the truth," he said at last. "You caught up with us."

"That wasn't what I meant. You are to replace the windows because you both were responsible for the willful destruction of them. Do you understand that?"

Both boys said they understood and Mr. Hanley told them to get back to their classes then, but for Queenie to wait another minute.

The boys left and Mr. Hanley explained, "Even though Persimmon hasn't reached high school yet, I've known him all these years. He hangs out in town and is something of a troublemaker, I've noticed. Also, he's lazy, and I couldn't believe he was way out at the end of town the day the church windows were broken unless he was up to some meanness. I questioned him then and again this morning, and there were too many discrepancies in his two versions of the incident. He tripped himself up, and I'm pleased that the whole matter is now closed. But it is unfortunate that you were . . . framed-up, I guess is the word."

"Yes, sir, that's the word," said Queenie.

"Of course, you have to admit your record of behavior hasn't been such that anyone was convinced it absolutely could not have been you. And you were within a stone's throw of real trouble, figuratively speaking. But if you'd learn to use your energy constructively, you might be surprised at how soon you would arrive at . . . well, let me put it this way: A decent, happy life is no more than a stone's throw away now, and it's up to you whether or not you get any nearer than that."

"I'll get nearer," said Queenie, sounding determined. "I'm gonna do better from now on."

"It seems you're already more cooperative. And in the face of your thinking you were leaving, I'm especially proud of you."

"I'm really going to cooperate now, Mr. Hanley, you wait and see. And I appreciate what you've done for me."

"You're very welcome," he said. "And just one more thing: I ran into Dr. Palmer in town and he said for you to drop by one day to talk about your part-time job." He smiled at her and added, "Who knows, you may grow up to be a nurse!"

Queenie smiled back. "I may grow up to be a doctor," she answered.

On the way home from school she went by Dr. Palmer's office. It was decided that she would work Saturdays, helping in the infirmary's kitchen at first, beginning in November. She thanked the doctor and then started home, singing "Listen to the Mockingbird" as she walked along. She couldn't remember when she had ever felt so good.

At the Evans' home beyond the town square, little Tilly popped out from behind one of the big oaks in the front yard and chanted:

> "Queenie's daddy's in the chain gang,
> Queenie's daddy's in the chain gang."

Then she hopped behind the tree again.

Queenie stopped singing. She felt her face grow warm, but quickly she relaxed. "That's all right, Tilly," she called. "You don't have to hide. I'm not going to throw a rock at you."

Tilly poked her head out. "How come?"

" 'Cause I've quit, that's how come."

"Aw, no!" said Tilly, as if she had been called on to give up her favorite pastime.

"And besides," said Queenie, starting ahead, "Pa's home now, didn't you know?"

She had already begun to sing again when behind her she heard Tilly's chant once more. The words had been changed slightly and did not fit the rhythm quite as well, but the cruelty of them was as clear as ever:

"Queenie's daddy *once was* in the chain gang,
Queenie's daddy *once was* in the chain gang."

Queenie did not stop or even turn around, but she quit singing. All of a sudden she didn't feel like singing. "The shadow of the jail!" she said to herself. "I'll always be in the shadow of the jail and there'll always be people around who won't want me to forget it." Then she remembered the advice Judge Lewis had given her— that she alone could decide whether she let it get her down. She could reason that nobody expected much of her, and not make any effort to succeed in life. But who would she be hurting in the long run?

"I'll succeed!" she said to herself so emphatically that she wondered if she had said it aloud. She was not at all sure she hadn't and looked around sheepishly to see if there happened to be anybody on the porches of the big houses, or in the yards, who might have heard her.

Then she went back to thinking: "I'll make something of myself! There's no telling what I can do if I try. Just you wait, Queenie Peavy, just you wait!" She knew she would always have to be reminding herself to control her temper, but she could learn to do that. She hadn't thrown a rock at Tilly the way she once would have. That was a beginning. And maybe folks who laughed at other people's misfortunes did really hurt themselves most of all. Surely sooner or later they would see how unfair they had been. Anyway, from now on she would tell herself "It's their own sadness instead of mine," the way Mr. Hanley had suggested.

She smiled when she realized what a lecture she had given herself. "I preached myself a sermon," she thought, "and the good part was that I listened." She admitted that most of it had been a rehashing of what grownups had tried to tell her all along.

How pleasant everything was going to be now! Her father was home, and she wasn't to be sent to the re-formatory—and for many reasons, she would become a new person. Singing at school the day before had been a start. Various people had paid her compliments about it—including Little Mother's brother Dave, who told her that he liked pretty singing a whole lot. And Cressie Whitfield said the songs beat anything she had ever heard on the radio, even programs from Nashville, Tennessee. Queenie thought of all the nice things that had happened and once again it was the happiest day of her life. She began to sing "What Can You Do with a Sawed-off Shovel?" and when she came to the "Dig, dig a hole" part, she broke into a springier step.

At home she hurried into the house. "Pa," she called, "are you here?"

No answer came and she rushed into the other room calling, "Where are you, Pa?" He was not there either, and she took her books and walked slowly to the yard, eating a biscuit she had filled with syrup.

Settling onto the big rock against the side of the chimney, her favorite study spot, she wrote fifteen English sentences for the next day and then read a chapter in the civics book. After a while Ol' Dominick strolled out from behind a clump of sedge brush, clucking noisily. "It *is not* time for me to shell the corn, I don't care what you say!" said Queenie, reaching out to the rooster. She petted him lovingly. "But if you'll stay with me while I run over my algebra problems, I'll feed you early, anyway." He went ahead with his clucking, as if he preferred special attention without delay. Queenie was laughing at him when her mother came into the yard.

"How come you're home so soon?" asked Queenie. "And where's Pa, is he with you?"

"No, he's not with me," said Mrs. Peavy, and she began to explain that part of the machinery at the canning plant had broken and the workers had been given the rest of the day off. "I stopped at Speer's and bought a stretch of cloth to sew you up a dress." She took the material from a paper bag.

"That's pretty," said Queenie, looking at the blue checkered gingham. "But I haven't outgrown this one I've got on, or my other one either."

Mrs. Peavy looked as if she were forcing herself to smile. "I'm going to make a little more money from now on," she said, "and maybe we can have a few things we don't absolutely require. Edna Boland left the plant to go to work in Griffin and I'm getting the job she gave up. And it pays more than my old one."

"Well, ain't we lucky!" said Queenie. "My goodness, when nice things begin to happen, there just doesn't seem to be any letup."

"Oh, there's a letup," said her mother, starting toward the backsteps. Her voice quavered slightly as she added, "Your Pa has broken parole. He waved a pistol in front of some folks and bragged that he would get even for deeds that should have been forgotten. He ought to have known they'd tell the sheriff."

"Aw heck!" said Queenie. "Why'd he go and do that? Reckon what they'll do to him?"

"They've already done it," her mother said softly. "They've taken him back to the penitentiary."

Walking to school the next morning, Queenie looked only at the ground until suddenly she lifted her head and said angrily, "I don't care! I don't care about anything—not anything in the world!" To convince herself that she meant it she gathered up a handful of stones and threw them at convenient targets: a fence post, the remains of a web left by tent caterpillars, and a tiny clump of mistletoe in a tall scarlet oak.

When she came to the Hilltop Baptist Church she had a single stone left. She looked up at the bell tower and saw that one little window, the highest one, had not been broken. "That Persimmon!" she thought. "He's a poor shot, but he could have kept trying till he knocked out that last pane. What was the sense of not doing the job right?" Then she remembered that the job she was thinking he should have done *right* had been *wrong* from the start. Maybe it was even *evil*, she decided, although she had never thought about what had to be worse than wrong to be considered evil.

She continued to look at the one unbroken pane. "I'll bet ol' Persimmon tried and tried to hit it," she said, smiling at the thought of him throwing rocks and missing. "I could hit it in one shot," she boasted to herself and drew back her arm, her fist clenching the stone that was left. But something stopped her. Words from her own lecture came back to her.

"But that was the other day," she argued, "and Pa was still at home. And now I don't care about anything!"

She took aim again, but her own voice nagged: "Just you wait, Queenie Peavy, just you wait! Go wild if you want to, see if I care! But who are you hurting in the long run?"

She lowered her arm and stood with her head down, thinking. Finally she unclenched her fist and looked at the rough stone that had almost broken a church window. "Go back to your friends!" she said, letting it drop to the ground. There it resembled any other rock on the roadside—except that its jagged edges reflected more sunlight.

Queenie Herself

Queenie's stone-throwing did not come to an altogether sudden end; she remained proud of her aim. But never again did she throw a rock just on an angry impulse. She was learning to think before acting, and she was learning to act wisely. And it surprised her to discover that she could face life as it was, instead of as she wished it to be, and have a good time too. Even when the truth was not easy to accept she was willing to try.

Also, she no longer felt deep resentment whenever people teased her. Sometimes she even laughed with them. However, she knew she would never have Little Mother's unbounded faith in human nature. When the two girls talked about the improvement in Cravey Mason's behavior, Little Mother was certain that the re-

sponsibility of being chairman of the social committee
had turned him into a new person. But Queenie
laughed. "He's probably as mean as ever," she said.

Before the eighth grade got around to having its
wiener roast, the ninth grade planned a party also. "And
Nash Parker invited me!" Little Mother told Queenie.
"He lives on the farm next to ours. And guess what! My
brother Dave wants you to be his guest!" Before
Queenie could say a word, Little Mother continued.
"Pa will take all of us in the wagon. Won't that be fun?
We can pick up Casey Pratt at Cross Creek and whoever he plans to invite—Kate Coogler, I think—and
we'll just have us a hay ride on the way to the party."
She added, with a giggle, "And I forgot, you're invited
to spend the night at our house. Mamma said I could
ask you." She repeated, "Won't it be fun?"

"It sure will!" agreed Queenie, and the day of the
party she was more certain of it than ever as she rode
home with Little Mother on the school bus. Dave rode
the bus, too, and sat on the back seat with some of his
friends. Queenie was careful not to turn around; she
didn't want him to think she was keeping an eye on
him.

At Little Mother's home, Mrs. Mullins greeted
Queenie cheerily. "Just be comfortable with us," she
said. "Pleasure yourself however you choose, and if you
want a job you can play with Burl while Martha and I
cook supper." She was looking at the baby, a smiling,
red-headed one holding onto the edge of a slatted crib.

"Isn't he sweet?" said Little Mother. "If you'd like to tote him around, he loves to go outside."

Queenie hated to say she didn't believe she'd ever held a baby that little, or that such things didn't appeal to her. Maybe he'll cry, she thought, and then somebody else can look after him. But instead he reached out to her, and she was surprised at how snugly he fitted into her arms—until he gave a jump and almost sprang out of them. She held him more firmly as she walked to the yard.

Two of the younger Mullins boys were at the steps, trying to make a whistle out of a piece of bamboo. They stopped to give Burl's toes a friendly tug and to let him pull their hair. He laughed when they laughed. Then Queenie took him across to where one of his sisters sat on top of a chicken coop, playing with a rag doll.

The older children were working. One boy was feeding hogs, and a girl was shelling corn for a flock of hens. Eleven-year-old Conroy took the two cows from the pasture to the barn and Queenie walked down to visit with him. "Burl likes to watch me milk," he said.

Before she could reply, a loud clanging noise caused her to turn around. Dave was driving a two-horse wagon out from the shed at the far end of the yard. He stopped in front of the barn. "I'll pitch down some straw for our hay ride," he explained, climbing up a ladder that was nailed to the wall.

Queenie thought of offering to help but decided she had better not. He might think that only boys should do heavy tasks. Anyhow, she would have had to take Burl back into the house, and she liked looking after him. So she stood in the doorway and let the baby watch Conroy milk while she watched Dave pitch hay from the loft. She was pleased at how strong and healthy he looked at work.

When he came down again, he stopped to rest. It was pleasant being near him, she thought, although neither he nor she seemed to know what to say. But Conroy helped them. "I'd let you try your hand at milking," he called to Queenie, as if he thought she never had seen a cow before. "But this new one is sort of jumpy and might haul off and kick you."

Queenie smiled. "I'd kick her back," she said, and both boys laughed at the joke their visitor had made. The baby laughed too, but he probably didn't know what was funny.